GODDESS SCORNED

GODDESS SCORNED

FORGOTTEN GODS, BOOK 2

ST BRANTON   CM RAYMOND   LE BARBANT

GODDESS SCORNED (this book) is a work of fiction.

All of the characters, organizations, and events portrayed in this novel are either products of the author's imagination or are used fictitiously. Sometimes both.

LMBPN Publishing
PMB 196, 2540 South Maryland Pkwy
Las Vegas, NV 89109

First US edition, March 2018
Version 1.01, March 2018

To Gavin, Hank, and Simone.
May you find magic everywhere and
causes worth fighting for.

1

THE THING about living like a rat in a maze was that you kind of get used to all the twists and turns. When you knew the labyrinth like the back of your hand, it was a lot less scary to run like hell through the dark. The narrow, grimy passages flashed by to the furious beat of my own footsteps. I could hear others behind me, closing in.

But I wasn't afraid.

In fact, a grin spread across my face as I careened around the last corner, the soles of my shoes skidding on the pavement. The dickheads chasing me down the alley didn't know it yet, but they were in for the surprise of their miserable lives.

They whooped triumphantly when they saw the dead end ahead. One of them even yelled out, "Stupid bitch!"

Typical.

The smile on my lips morphed into one of satisfaction. I slipped my hand into the bag flapping at my side, closing my fingers around the familiar weight of a certain sword hilt. No doubt word of Kronin's blade had made its way around whatever underground circles these toothy dipshits ran in, but it didn't matter if they knew I had it.

They would die all the same.

A wall of old brick came rushing at me as I skidded to a stop. I narrowly avoided it before spinning on my heels to face the goon squad. To anyone else, they might have looked almost normal, if exceptionally ugly, but I was getting pretty good at picking the vamps out of a crowd. Then again, they were usually looking for me, too. So, maybe I had an unfair advantage.

"I don't know what the hell you were thinking," one of them growled. The points of his teeth glinted from beneath thin, pale lips. He was gaunt, his skin a grimy, sick grey. "But you sure know how to work up my appetite."

"Sorry, sweetie," I said in the most saccharine, insulting tone I could manage. "I'm not on the menu tonight." My grip tightened on the hilt of the sword.

Showtime.

Loosing the weapon from the confines of my bag, I willed its brilliant blade into existence. The narrow alley filled with its burning golden light. Heat washed over my skin. The vamp's hungry eyes tracked the edge of the sword for a split second. Then, his lips peeled back from the fangs entrenched in his gums.

I might have thought they were fake if I didn't know otherwise.

He was fast, but they all were, and after two weeks of dealing with their monster bullshit, the speed was something my reflexes were learning to handle. Plus it helped that I was slightly more than human now.

Not only did I have *Gladius Solis*, the sword of the gods, but I had also tasted nectar from Carcerum. Marcus used it to save my life, but it gave me so much more than that. It gave me the strength to curb stomp this vampire and his shitty crew.

But they might be able to tell me something interesting.

Shifting my weight backward, I raised Kronin's sword at an angle just as the lead vamp pushed off into a charging leap. His shadow fell over me, and when I craned my neck back to keep an eye on his progress, I met a ruthless, predatory stare. He obviously thought I was about to die.

They always did.

Instead of dying, I caught him in the sternum, driving the point of the sword between his outstretched hands. He managed to latch onto me for a moment, just long enough for his clawed nails to rip through the shoulder of my already beat-up sweater. I pushed the hilt forward as gravity drew him farther down the blade. He flung himself backward. His twitching limbs struck out at his friends, but they let him fall to the concrete.

No loyalty among the undead.

The other four had formed a semicircle around me, so close that I smelled their dry, rotten breath. Their sharp eyes gleamed in the dark, even above the sword's golden glow. The one in front of me licked his lips.

"You have a strong heart," he said. "I like that in my prey."

I scowled. These guys made killing a lot more satisfying than it had any right to be. "I've got a strong swing, too. Let me demonstrate."

The blade cut a gorgeous arc through the steadily deepening shadows. My target ducked, but one of his friends wasn't so quick or lucky. The rush of the strike gave way to the sound of a head coming to rest somewhere down the alley. Its former body collapsed like a sandbag, spilling coarse dust around our feet.

The three remaining closed in tighter around me. A pair of hands grabbed for my throat, and the long edge of a nail grazed my neck. The vampire's grip closed down, and a shot of adrenaline raced through my veins as I realized I couldn't breathe.

Concentrate, Victoria. Steel your nerves,

Marcus' voice snapped me back into the present. The gears in my mind stopped grinding. Pushing off the wall at my back, I rammed the sword forward with all the strength I could muster. It didn't matter where it went. They were so close it was bound to hit someone. There was little resistance, but the telltale gurgling told me I was right.

As the latest casualty began to dissolve around the brand new hole in his stomach, I caught a fistful of his crumbling corpse and threw it at the others. They raised their arms to shield their bulbous eyes, and I took the opportunity to level the playing field. I swung low, cutting off one vamp at the knees. The other reached for me and I severed his arms in one clean chop. On the ground, these dudes were a lot less intimidating. I hadn't been scared of them since learning they could still feel pain.

The one farthest from me tried to crawl away on what was left of his legs, wheezing and cursing under his breath. I caught up with him in two steps and planted my foot squarely on his back. He half twisted to look up at me, squinting in the glare of the sword.

"Let me go, bitch," he coughed. "What's a guy with no arms gonna do?"

"Die," I shrugged. Another hard punch, and the sword went through him as if he wasn't even there. Pretty soon, he wasn't anything more than a vague depression left in the pavement by the force of the killing blow. I walked back to the lone survivor, smiling. "Congratulations, dickwad. You're the last vamp lying down. I guess that means you win."

"You heathen whore," he spat. The ragged lump of flesh that used to be his arm twitched and stretched, trying to regrow. I still had time—grievous injuries like those took longer to mend than a paper cut—unless he could find someone to feed on. "You ain't getting nothing from me."

"That's interesting." I knelt on his chest, bearing down with the point of my knee until he gasped. "Because I'm thinking you're gonna sing like a canary."

He spat for real this time, into my face. So, I forced his mouth open with the butt of the sword hilt and used it to crush one of his fangs from its socket. He made a muffled cry, underscored by the crack of bone. A network of veins spidered over his temples and down his neck.

When I pulled the sword out of his craw, he just glared. "Suck me off, you ravening wh—."

I crushed the other fang before he could finish his insult. "Don't push it, pal. This sword kills gods. What do you think it would do to you?"

There were jagged gaps in his grin when he laughed. "You think that's the only thing that can kill gods? There's other power out there—we'll have a light of our own soon. Then, you'll get what's coming to you."

I kept my expression neutral. "Where's your boss?"

That was all I really needed to know. Ever since the operation inside the old slaughterhouse had been shut down, I hadn't seen hide nor hair of Lorcan or his cronies —which made me more than a little nervous. At this point, I knew better than to assume they were gone for good.

"I gotta give it to you," said the vamp, his voice hoarse from the pressure on his chest. "You got some real high hopes. When *he* finds you, he'll do worse than bleed you dry. His powers are beyond the comprehension of even the smartest humans. Your world will die screaming in darkness."

"Not before you do." I replaced my knee with the sword, pushing down until I felt the ground beneath his body. He took one last breath before his eyes rolled up.

Ten seconds later, I stood alone in a graveyard full of stony ashes, the sword hilt stashed away in my bag. The ever-present ambience of New York traffic hummed some-where beyond the alley's walls. It was a far better sound than the ravings of a dying vampire, but a certain Roman centurion had taught me not to discount such things off the bat. Which reminded me.

"How'd I do?" I asked the medallion that now housed the spirit of my former fighting partner. The arrangement was a little weird, but growing on me. Like a louder, more persistent conscience.

Victoria! Why would you put the Gladius Solis *inside the mouth of a cursed lowlife?* the old soldier demanded imme-diately.

"Cut me some slack, Marcus, okay? I wanted to see if

this thing could make him talk. Besides, I'm sure the sword of a hero god has seen worse than a little vampire spit."

That is a fair assessment. But such a weapon deserves to be handled with a little more decorum, don't you think?

I smiled slightly. Marcus's near-fanatical devotion to this thing was bizarrely endearing. "Okay, okay. I'll use some Lysol when we get home. He didn't have shit to say anyway."

Following the sound of traffic, I started to make my way out of the filthy labyrinth, but a weird feeling nagged at the corners of my mind, like I was forgetting something. I glanced over my shoulder, but there was nothing behind me except five inconspicuous piles of dust.

Then I pulled my phone out and saw what time it was. "Oh, balls. I have to run."

Why? Marcus asked. *You do not have an occupation.*

"No, dude." I broke into a sprint. "I forgot I was supposed to meet Jules for drinks."

Ah, drinking. Marcus's words took on a wistful note. *One of the things I miss the most about residing on a physical plane. Sometimes, being your passenger has considerable drawbacks.*

He went on, but I tuned him out so I could focus on coming up with an excuse for my lateness that Jules might actually believe. She'd always been able to see straight through my bullshit, but I thought if she knew what was really going on with me, her head might explode.

Lying made me feel bad, but some secrets—like mine— were just too big to tell.

2

"Hey!" Jules waved to me from a corner table inside the tidy little bar she'd chosen as our meeting place. It was a far cry from the seedy dives I was used to, and I had to admit it was a nice change of pace.

I slid into the seat across from her.

"I was beginning to wonder if you forgot about me," she said.

"Sorry," I said sheepishly. "Kind of got caught up in something."

The bar's décor was suddenly the most interesting thing in the world to me as I braced myself for Jules's inevitable barrage of questions. These days, she was used to not taking me at my word, and to be fair, I could hardly blame her.

She just shrugged and studied the wine list. "You sound like me at work," she said, chuckling. "I'm always getting lost in one thing or another. That's what I get for trying to practice law in the city that never sleeps."

"Hey, I tried to tell you it was nuts to go to law school, but you wouldn't listen. Something about 'making the world a better place.'" I was kidding, of course. If public defense had a face, it was Jules Lugnor. There was no one more selfless and giving in the world.

"I'm working on it." Her voice had a weird edge, an undercurrent of something indistinguishable. After a moment of silence, she looked up at me and smiled. "But that's nothing new. You want to hear something *really* crazy?" Jules leaned across the table, so I did too. "This needs to stay on the down low, obviously."

"Right." A conspiratorial little smirk crept across my lips. We all like to think we're above gossip past the age of twenty, and she was probably breaking at least one law every time she told me something, but I secretly delighted in the things she shared. Plus, it gave me a way to see into her world, which was usually so far removed from my own.

Not this time.

"There's been talk around the office." She was whispering now. "You heard about what the police found in the Meatpacking District a couple of weeks ago, right?"

"I think so, yeah." Understatement of my lifetime.

"Well, a girl came in to speak to an attorney last week. She had a story to tell, but she didn't think the police would believe her."

"And she decided to talk to a public defender? Isn't that, like, weird?"

"A little, maybe. But it could be smart, depending on what she had to say. And it let her take advantage of attorney-client privilege."

It was a risk to sound too eager, but I really wanted to know what Jules was getting at. Maybe this girl knew more about Lorcan's current whereabouts. "That sounds like it could be pretty crazy. I hope everything shakes out all right."

Victoria. Perhaps the girl of which Jules speaks is one of the women you rescued from the cage. Marcus's voice interrupted my thoughts, and even though I agreed with him, I frowned a little bit. I still wasn't quite used to the sudden intrusion of someone else's consciousness in my ears. The urge to shush him out loud was nearly overwhelming.

"We'll see." Jules took a sip of her drink and looked at me closely. "Wasn't that right around the time I had to bail you and a certain someone out of jail?" Her mouth smiled, but her eyes narrowed slightly. "You wouldn't happen to know anything about it, would you?"

I blinked, then forced a laugh. "Me? Of course not, Jules. Come on." I made sure not to protest too much, lest she become suspicious. "The Meatpacking District's all trendy now. We both know I can't afford that shit."

She was silent for two beats, apparently scrutinizing me. Then she laughed, and the sound broke the subtle tension that had begun to form between us. "Relax, Vic! I'm only kidding. Your friend was wearing armor, for Pete's sake. Pretty sure the media would've jumped all over a guy in that kind of getup." Her perfectly arched brows knit together. "What happened to him, anyway? Still bumming it out at your place?"

"No," I said, maybe too fast. "He decided to move on a while ago." For effect, I shrugged. "He was kind of a drifter, I think. Bit of a douche really."

I am no such thing. Marcus interjected. *I am a warrior.*

"So he just left?" Jules gave me a look. "Where exactly is he going to go?"

It was my turn to look at her. "What do you mean?" I'd expected her to chuckle, shrug it off, and maybe express the hope that he landed on his feet. But she seemed to be focused on it, waiting expectantly for my answer. "How the hell should I know?"

My glass landed back on the table a little more heavily than intended. She was making me nervous.

"Just curious. It looked like you two got along pretty well. I would have assumed he'd leave you a forwarding address or something."

There is no need for this "forwarding address," said Marcus cheerfully. *You have inherited my family's medallion, and thus, you have custody of my spirit. It is an honor.*

At the moment, it didn't really feel like one. The beginnings of a headache were putting down roots in my temples.

"I don't think he has one," I told Jules lamely, desperate to change the subject. "Want me to go get us another round?"

She cast a glance over toward the bar. "Yeah, why not? There's a guy up there who's been checking you out since we got here. Maybe you can make a new friend."

I believe your life would be positively enhanced by the addition of more friends.

"No thanks. I've got enough men in my life as it is." Grabbing both my glass and Jules's, I headed up to the bar and set them in front of the bartender. "Can I get a refill?"

He gave me a friendly smile. "Sure. Give me just a second."

It made me uneasy to stand with my back to the whole room, so I sank strategically down on one of the barstools to wait, scanning the area. Everyone in there was dressed better than me, drinking in dresses and button-downs, with phones and jewelry on full display. From a security standpoint, the finery didn't make me feel better.

Rocco and his ilk had nice things, too.

But if they had gold watches, I had a sword, and I was pretty sure that would give me the edge if some shit happened to go down. Bringing this particular sword to a gun fight no longer made me nervous.

Be at peace, Victoria. There are no threats here. Even without a body, Marcus's smirk was audible in my mind. *The amorous gentleman at the end of the bar is keen to make your acquaintance, judging by the way he keeps turning toward us. Perhaps you ought to take Jules's advice.*

"No." My voice stayed low. It was still strange to talk to Marcus out loud, but he couldn't read my mind, which was both good *and* bad. "And how do you know there are no threats here? Can you read minds or something?"

I am simply both observant and experienced, if you must know. And besides, this location is much too refined for the likes of any underling. And if Lorcan himself were here, I'm sure I would know.

"And you'd tell me, right?"

Of course.

Out of the corner of my eye, I saw my would-be admirer start to slide off his stool and approach me. He might've given me Deacon flashbacks if he were even half as attractive. "Shit."

"That guy isn't coming to give you trouble, is he?" The bartender had returned with fresh drinks while I was preoccupied.

I turned to him, willing my nerves to steady up so that the drinks didn't spill everywhere. "Ah, no. I was just leaving anyway." Then I scuttled back to the table where Jules was waiting, an amused smirk on her face. I put her martini in front of her. "Don't you say a damn word. Just drink."

Jules swirled her olives around the glass, examining me again. "You know, I seem to recall you having a different attitude toward meeting boys in bars during college," she said slyly.

This sounds like a tale I would very much like to hear.

Burying my face in my hands, I groaned. "Let's not do this right now."

I disagree. Let us proceed. Marcus's invisible grin only widened with every passing second.

"Is it Ezra's friend?" Jules prodded, somewhat gleeful. "What's his name? The cop?"

"First of all, he's FBI. He made it a point to let me know."

"Ooh, spooky." Another sip of the martini disappeared behind her lips. She was obviously enjoying this torment of my soul, and I couldn't really blame her. It had been a long time since we'd last been able to just hang out as friends.

But she was really digging in here. "Second, I can't believe you already forgot his name. You met him like a week ago. It's Deacon."

"Right." She shrugged in a *sue-me* kind of gesture. "I know so many law enforcement guys, Vic. He'll have to stand out if he wants me to remember him."

"What?" I asked. "His face isn't enough?"

"Aha!" Jules slapped the table. "You do like him! I knew it!" Her giant smile was so infectious that I found myself returning it across the table.

"Shut up. I never said that. I plead the fifth." A blush threatened to creep up into my cheeks, but I forced it down through sheer willpower. I'd never hear the end of it if she saw me blushing over Deacon.

"That's total crap, and you know it," Jules said. "You're incapable of physical attraction unless you like the guy too."

Glancing away, I took a deep, purposeful pull from my beer. "This conversation is turning into slander."

Jules rolled her blue eyes. "Would you stop being so defensive? I'm happy for you! I haven't seen you exercise this much emotional capability since…" She trailed off, and we both were quiet for a minute. "I'm sorry," she said at last. "I shouldn't have—"

"Don't worry about it." But the seed of melancholy had been planted, and in my tipsy state, I felt it spreading. The rest of my beer went down in one swallow. "I should go, though. I've got some stuff to take care of."

"Okay." She sighed, got up from her seat, and put her arms around me for a big squeeze. "Look after yourself, Vic. And don't be a stranger. I'm always here for you."

"I know." The only smile I managed this time was a little bit sad. "Thanks, Jules. I'll see you later."

She didn't offer to walk out with me.

3

Marcus was quiet for a while as I walked down Brooklyn side streets, winding my way toward a destination he didn't know. My feet walked themselves through the dusky shadows of New York's night. They knew where we were going, even if my heart didn't want to admit it.

You never told me much about your past adventures.

I ran my fingers along the medallion's chain. The feel of its gold links soothed me somehow. "I bet you wish she would've finished that story, huh?"

Personally, I was glad she hadn't. Hearing about myself from back then, before life had broken into a million unrecognizable pieces, still hurt—not as much as it used to, but a little more than I wanted to admit. It just made the "what-ifs" start full force in my brain.

What if my parents were still alive? What if I lived in a real house and had a real job, and lived a real, normal life?

What if none of this had ever happened?

I will always be interested to hear of your life, should you choose to share it with me. We are family now, after all.

The medallion warmed against my skin as if to let me know that Marcus was there, walking in spirit beside me. Closing my hand around the chain, I shut my eyes and took a deep breath.

"Maybe someday. Not today." It took me a second to choose the next words carefully. "When we get to where we're going, I'm gonna take this off, okay? I'll put it back on when I'm done. I promise. I just need to be alone for a while."

I always felt a shade of guilt whenever I removed Marcus from my neck, essentially cutting him off from my plane of existence. It was hard to imagine what that was like for him. Then again, we hadn't become one person after he died. I was still entitled to all the privacy in the world. Maybe it just felt weird to be so totally in control of something.

For once.

Take whatever time you need. I will be here when you are ready.

Marcus could be annoying. He could be worse as a voice in my head than he ever was in the short days he spent by my side. But he remained steadfast, and he had a knack for finding the right words to say.

That was all I could ask for, really. And he was right—the dead Centurion was the only family I had.

The medallion sat heavy in my right pocket as I crept down the row in Cypress Hills, picking through the darkness for the all-too-familiar marker in the ground. It was flat and tidy, and it bore nothing but their names. Edward and Loretta Stratton, born apart, died together.

"Hey, guys." I knelt carefully in the grass beside the marker, brushing stray specks of dirt and grass from the simple engraving. It had been all I could afford inside such a famous cemetery, but more than that, I wanted their resting place to match who they were. Humble, sweet, kind, and settled down in a world much, much bigger than them.

The silence in a graveyard has its own texture, its own soft weight. In the days when my loss was still fresh, I'd come to Cypress Hills a lot just to sit in front of the plot and cry, shielded by the somber stillness. It was the one place where I was never bothered. No one gave me a second thought, but at least, in the cemetery, they gave me space.

I breathed in the cool night air and shut my eyes. Memories—some vivid, some vague—slipped through my mind, one after the other. There I was, coloring at the kitchen table with Mom, scribbling a new set of crayons down to nubs. There was Mom, tucking me into bed, leaning over to kiss my forehead the way she did every single night. I smelled her mint and lavender soap.

"I love you, Victoria," she'd whispered.

And then I saw Dad launching me down the street in front of our house at a run, pushing the bike forward with all his might, yelling, "Pedal, Victoria, pedal! You can do it!"

His voice was stronger than Marcus's.

A tear sneaked out the corner of my eye and rolled down my cheek, pulling me back to the present. Even with my eyes open, Dad's voice echoed from the past, full of hope and promise.

"I don't know, Dad," I said softly. The grave marker blurred, and a sigh escaped me. "I started all of this for you, for you and Mom. Now it's so much bigger than all of us. You taught me to be strong and I am, but is that strength enough to level against the gods?" No answer, of course. So I provided my own. "It'll have to be."

I had spent so long thinking that Rocco Durant was my endgame, that everything would sort itself out once he was dead. Then I learned about the gods. Now, I was barreling down a whole different warpath, one that I hadn't even had the luxury of choosing for myself. But sometimes, the most important paths chose you.

I traced the letters of my parents' names with my finger. It was difficult not to wonder how they might have felt if they could see me now. The hunt for justice had made me a criminal, and it had stained my hands with blood and ash. It was a far cry from taking up the family business of check cashing, or whatever the hell they wanted my life to be.

Stability? None. A roof over my head? Technically. A warm, loving family environment? Well, I had an ancient soldier in a pendant around my neck.

The breeze sifted through my hair, bringing me back to my bike in the street and Dad running behind me. He was still shouting. "Pedal! Pedal! You can do it!" And as I went sailing over the pavement on my own for the first time, he let out a whoop of unfiltered joy. "Yes! Look at you go!"

Instead of crying, I smiled this time. Maybe I *could* stand in the face of the gods. Luck hadn't been on my side in five years, but strength and determination were solidly in my corner. If I could take down a mob-boss-turned-vampire, I sure as hell could keep moving forward to see what the gods had in store.

The sword hilt shifted in my bag as I got to my feet. I patted it and blew a kiss to my parents. The flower stand beside their plot stood empty. "I'll bring some next time," I said sheepishly. "I'm a little short on cash right now."

Hail, Victoria. The medallion settled in its customary position against my sternum. It warmed each time Marcus spoke, sort of like a weird little heartbeat. He didn't ask about where I'd been, or why I required privacy. I didn't tell him.

"I've made a decision," I declared, leaving the iron fences of Cypress Hills behind me. "Obviously there are things that need to be done, and I'm the one to do them, for better or worse. Whatever the gods are planning, we're gonna get to the bottom of it. But I'll need your help."

Were you not fully committed before? He was not hurt or accusatory, only curious.

"I mean, I sort of didn't have a choice, dude. It was either get involved or let you drown in the river. We've talked about this."

True. I have always been an excellent recruiter.

"Very funny. But seriously, what's our next move?" The grimy, fangless face of the vamp I'd dispatched before meeting Jules flashed in my mind's eye. "We've been chasing these bloodsucking douchebags for weeks, and I feel like we're just running in place."

Things have been conspicuously slow, he admitted. *I too had hoped another clear avenue would have presented itself by now.*

I ran a hand through my hair. "It's just—if I'm going to save the world, I need to know what kinds of threats I'm facing. Seems only fair."

I only wish I could direct you exactly, but I'm afraid the whims of the gods are fickle. The sole constant is crushing war. Which will mean more or less total annihilation for humans. They are being very serious when they speak of world domination.

"Basically, you're saying they just want to screw us over any way they can." I frowned. "Wow. Love that."

No. They want to own this planet like they used to. Screwing you over is simply a fringe benefit. He paused. *You will need to improve your performance if you want to have any hope of stopping them. There was a close call in the alley earlier. If I did not know better, I might think you were getting sloppy.*

"What? Come on. It's been a couple weeks at most. How can I already be getting sloppy?"

Good question. You are fortunate to have made excellent friends with a Roman centurion, then.

I groaned, suddenly anticipating many more blasphemously early mornings spent swinging at the air with a sword. "Okay, okay. I'll do better. But we need more than just practice. I can get as kickass as I want, and we'll still be shit out of luck without any leads. I'm tired of waiting for their next attack. It's time to try taking the offensive."

4

I DRAGGED myself out of bed before dawn the next morning, maneuvering gingerly around the curled-up cat who lay purring in the center of the blankets. A splash of freezing water shocked the fog from my brain. One pair of sweatpants and a torn sweatshirt later, I slipped the medallion over my head. "Hey. You ready?"

I don't really sleep anymore, so yes, I'm ready. Are you?

"I don't get any readier than this."

A pair of filled water drums, the big kind made for office coolers, rested near the foot of my bed. As a pre-training exercise to get me in the right mindset, I had taken to lifting these things in lieu of actual weights. I held each one of them over my head, pausing long enough that my arms begin to burn, before I slowly eased them down until they were parallel with the floor. The muscles in my back and throughout the rest of my core woke up and shouted at me.

"You know what I really like?" I said, to no one in

particular. "Being strong enough to do this kind of crap!" I found it both exhilarating and empowering.

Not bad...for an amateur.

"Dude." I laughed a little breathlessly as I did another rep. The water sloshed and I slowed my pace, focusing on control. "Let me have this."

But military pressing water wasn't the main objective—just a little diversion I used to stoke the fires of confidence at whatever ungodly hour it was. Once the jugs had come back to rest on the floor of the loft, it was time to get down to business.

Bending over, I picked up a training sword that was missing a big chunk of the blunt blade. "Remind me to find some replacements for these. We really did a number on them."

A worthwhile sacrifice. Your sword work is improving. I'd rate it a hair above terrible now.

I rolled my eyes, then got to work. The busted training blade still created a satisfying whish through the air when I swung it. I had to hold it tighter than usual so its unbalanced weight wouldn't send it careening out of my hand. The loft—and my furniture—still bore the scars of my very first vampire encounter. The last thing I needed was to wreck my own place all over again.

Fortunately, my warm-up drills were becoming second nature. The act of swinging had been transformed from an awkward, clumsy movement to something approaching gracefulness. I still didn't look half as cool or majestic as Marcus cutting down goons five minutes after being pulled from the river, but at least progress was being made.

I never thought I'd be proud of my swordsmanship someday.

Good. Watch your feet. A clever opponent will exploit your balance to his own advantage.

Of course, it helped that I had Marcus talking in my ear. How many people can say they've been trained by a Roman centurion?

"Can I ask you something?" I stepped forward, twirled, and brought the training sword down in a slashing arc.

Anything. As long as you mind your feet.

"Uh huh. How often did Kronin actually need to use his sword?" He fell silent. "Be honest, Marcus."

After the war, sightings of the Gladius Solis *were rare. The gods' great violence took on a different, more subtle nature once they were banned to Carcerum. Acts of deceit, subterfuge, espionage. Even in a realm of peace and beauty, their thirst for power couldn't be satisfied.*

"They sound like us. But how many times did you personally see Kronin use this thing?" Jabbing at the air, I envisioned the spot where a vampire's heart would be.

Once. Marcus paused. Something I wasn't used to. The day he died.

"Lucky him."

You are not living in times of peace, and you do not carry the authority of the greatest being who ever lived. Now, picture your foe before you.

"Already on it." Rocco Durant's ugly mug was still my default as far as the face of my worst enemy went. Some part of my brain had a hard time processing the fact that he was gone, that I had really killed him. Obviously, there had been other fights since then, during which I'd seen other vamps, but Rocco's death remained surreal.

Maybe because in my mind, destroying him had always meant freedom. And I wasn't free. If anything, I was in deeper than ever.

My foot slipped, and the training sword clattered to the floor. "Shit."

Focus, Victoria. A wandering mind leads to a weak blade.

"Sorry." Shaking it off, I lifted the weapon, which felt way lighter than it used to. Yeah, it was missing a piece, but I was also stronger now, and faster. Another reason I had to be extra careful training in the loft. That sorry excuse for a punching bag wouldn't cut it anymore.

Tell me what is on your mind. Perhaps I can ease your burden.

"Not much." It was a blatant lie, given that he had just witnessed me tripping over nothing. As if to prove my point, I wound up for a charging strike, leapt forward, and promptly broke another splinter off the edge of the wooden trainer.

Not much, Marcus repeated. For a guy who was thousands of years old, he had a surprisingly firm grasp of sarcasm.

"Okay, okay. Let me take five." I laid down the broken sword and trudged over to my mattress. The cat yawned as I sat down next to her, waking her up. "It's just, the sword still doesn't feel quite right. How did he used to use it to subdue the gods when I still feel like a kid trying on my mom's shoes when I'm swinging it around, you know? It doesn't feel like I'm ready to face off against someone else who doesn't just have a shitty gun."

Funny how a few fights with Kronin's sword had changed my opinion of firearms so thoroughly.

Marcus laughed. *All warriors feel this way at the beginning. The ones who say they do not are liars. I was like you once.*

"How do I get past it?" My fingers scratched behind the cat's soft ears. "If I go out there feeling like this, I'm gonna get my ass kicked. We both know that."

But do you have these doubts in the heat of a fight?

I took a minute to think about that one. The conclusion was pleasantly surprising. "Not really. I gotta say, wielding this thing is a real confidence-booster."

I am sure Kronin would agree with you. He paused. *It is also true that you have not yet unlocked the blade's full potential—at least according to the legends. I figured it would come to you when the time was right, but perhaps you require a nudge in the right direction. Go retrieve it, and we will try something new.*

Grabbing the *Gladius Solis* from its resting place against the wall by the bed, I stood up and walked to the center of the room. My body automatically arranged itself into a fighting stance with the weapon out in front. Insecurities aside, I'd be lying if I said it didn't feel at least a little bit awesome every time. There was just something about that sword.

Dare I say magical?

Throw it.

I hesitated, unsure if Marcus had actually said that. "Excuse me?"

Throw the sword. Not hard. At the bed.

This was *definitely* above my level. I couldn't imagine a scenario in which throwing my only real weapon would end well, but I forced myself to trust Marcus and do what I was told. Conscientiously avoiding the cat, I tossed the sword hilt onto the mattress. Its weight sagged the edges down. The cat meowed accusingly. "Sorry, cutie," I said. "Marcus made me do it for reasons he hasn't told me yet."

Kronin had the ability to call the Gladius Solis *when he needed it or when it was out of his reach. This was exceedingly useful to him over the duration of the war, and I suspect it will be helpful to you as well, provided you can learn the technique.*

"What's the technique?" I couldn't resist a smirk. "Do a headstand in a swamp? Wear a cape and become the god of thunder?"

Truly, your wit grows every day. No. Just hold out your hand and call.

"Like, out loud?" Still smiling, I held my hand palm out. "*Gladius Solis?*"

Nothing.

Marcus sighed. *You must command it, Victoria. You are not asking permission. The sword must know to work in concert with you.*

With the smile forcibly wiped off my face, I refocused my mental energy on the hilt. "*Gladius Solis.*"

This time, the sword twitched where it lay. The bedsheets shifted a little.

Try again.

I cleared my throat and imagined the sword as mine and no one else's. Kronin, Hero-King of the Gods? Just some dude who got wrecked by his ex-best-friend. It was all about me now. "*Gladius Solis!*"

The sword lurched off the bed and hit the floor with a loud, heavy thud. I winced. The cat sprang up, her tail puffed all the way out. She hissed.

Hmm. Marcus said. *I think this will take some work.*

"Yeah, I'll just plan on holding on to this thing for now." I rescued the hilt from the floor and leaned it back in its place. "Maybe I'm not cut out for mind tricks."

It is not a mind trick. The wielder fosters a connection with the sword which can manifest on demand.

"Well, I think the cat is traumatized." I reached to pet her, and she ducked away from my hand, eyes wide and staring. "Yep. That's the face of someone who's gonna need therapy. Vic the Bold, defender of the world, terrorizer of small furry mammals. It has a certain ring to it."

I'll be sure to alert the bards.

I could almost feel his nonexistent eyes rolling.

DAWN BROKE as my skillet sizzled on the hot plate, full of the last eggs and bacon in my otherwise empty fridge. I'd been trying to do better about stealing ever since I'd come to grips about my place in the new cosmic order. It didn't exactly feel right to be pickpocketing at the same time as I was trying to save the world.

Then again, I had to eat. And no one was going to pay me a living wage to do the shit I had to do.

"What's next?" I poked at the eggs with a spoon. Things had been relatively quiet up until the night before, and it was starting to make me antsy. The bastards had been running a regular vampire factory in the Meatpacking District, and given the scale of that operation, I was willing to bet it wasn't the only one they had. They weren't going to quit just because some girl got under their skin.

Even if that girl was carrying a god-king's sword.

No, they were up to something for sure. I just didn't know what, and for once, I couldn't beat it out of anyone.

You were correct last night. It is past time we change our approach if we want to make a real difference in the wars to come.

"You mean I have to stop punching people and stabbing them with a big-ass knife?" I made a big, dramatic sigh. "Fine. It hasn't done me much good so far anyway. Though I have to say, I've gotten pretty damn good at it."

Your pride is not necessarily misplaced, but I must inform you that not all minions of the gods will be so easy to vanquish. Lorcan is simply economizing his power, for now. When the time comes, be certain that neither he nor any of his counterparts will show anything close to mercy.

"Oh yeah?" Thinking he was just trying to counter my inclination toward cockiness, I goaded him a little further. "What sort of fun am I signing myself up for, here? You know all kinds of crazy legends, don't you? Which ones are true?"

Marcus hesitated. *Most of them. All those you can remember, anyway. The gods look like beasts, and they look like people. They are beautiful as often as they are frightening. And they are all gathering their own armies as we speak. It is true that some will be more formidable than others, but altogether, they are not to be taken lightly. A thousand humans are no match for even the weakest of gods—and when they start fighting each other, they will carry no concern for collateral damage.*

"Then why are we just sitting here?" I asked impatiently. "You may not have noticed, but there are more than a thousand humans around. We could start...assembling or something. Better than waiting around to get steamrolled by a bunch of supernatural warring dickheads." I tested the eggs. Still hot.

I know that this will not appeal to your brash, impulsive nature, Victoria, but we are currently doing all we can. For now, we are on damage control only. Hunt down the fires, put them out, wait for new ones to arise. It is too dangerous to your credibility if you attempt a preemptive strike before the gods make themselves known.

"You're saying no one will believe me." I knew he was telling the truth, but he was right; I didn't like it.

Precisely. Your powers of comprehension continue to impress me.

"Hey, I'm trying my best."

The vamps were ugly, boorish, greedy sons of bitches, but they were not snitches. It would be no skin off my back to keep killing them until something turned up, but Marcus's point was well taken. More than likely, all we'd get from a bloody rampage was a trail of bodies.

And that was something I couldn't afford.

But there is something we can do. We need to move our attention toward gathering intelligence instead. The servants of Lorcan aren't talking, but there are others who might. Perhaps more information will provide a lead.

"Sounds good to me." Breakfast sat cooling for approximately thirty more seconds before I shoveled it into my mouth straight from the pan. "Okay, let's get out of here. If we're looking for dirt, I know exactly where to start."

5

Mac sat with his feet propped up on a stool behind his stand, chewing gum and paging through a paper. His wrinkled face broke into a toothy grin when he saw me come up to the counter.

"Well, if it ain't Vic! Good to see ya, kiddo. I was beginning to think you moved or something!"

I smiled. "Sorry, Mac. I've been laying low for a bit, but I knew you'd do okay without me." My glance ran over the periodicals lined up neatly in the front rack of the newsstand.

No crimes in the front-page headlines, a rarity in and of itself. And nothing in the tabloids that sounded like it might apply to any real-world situation I knew of. The monsters on my shit list weren't invading from space—they were already here.

I just needed to hunt them down.

Mac frowned at me, the lines around his mouth deepening. "Don't tell me you're in trouble, Vic. You're just keeping your head down because you know what's good for you, right?"

I gave him a cheeky wink. "More or less. You won't worry if I don't give you details."

He shook his head. "Then I won't ask. The worrying is non-negotiable, though. That's gonna happen whether you like it or not." He slapped a paper down in front of me and added a pack of gum. "Here. For you, a quarter special."

Fifty cents made the trek across the counter. "Keep the change. Thanks, Mac."

I tucked the newspaper under my arm, pocketed the gum, and turned around, just another satisfied customer.

Good thing, too, because the next face I saw belonged to a certain smooth-talking FBI agent. And he was not alone.

"Damn it," I whispered.

What is the problem? Marcus, who'd been silent as a lamb at the newsstand, suddenly jumped in on high alert.

Sucking in my breath, I hissed, "Don't startle me like that! Deacon's over there. I need to be invisible."

The woman walking with Deacon St. Clare had a severe, sharply angled face that was only emphasized by the tightness of her pulled-back hair. She was the epitome of no-nonsense, dressed in exactly the same shade of black from head to toe, except for a crisp white blouse under her blazer. Her eyes snapped around like lasers, looking for something.

Prey, most likely.

Deacon ambled along beside her, keeping an eye on the side of the pavement that was closest to him, which just so happened to be the side I was on. It was too late to hide behind the newspaper; he'd notice that immediately. I turned my face away and increased my pace to a power-walk, heading down toward the nearest alley. Unfortunately, that alley was behind me, and Deacon saw me turn around.

"Hey, Vic."

I heard him but didn't stop. Just short of a jog, I slipped between the buildings and aimed for the fence at the end. It was sort of tall but flat on the top. A feasible two-handed vault.

This agent knows nothing of the sword. He cannot connect you to piles of ash on the streets. I fear you will only draw suspicion by fleeing.

"If he doesn't catch me, it won't matter, will it?" I hooked my fingers over the top of the fence and began to pull myself up. Halfway over, I heard Deacon's voice at a distance behind me.

"Don't worry about it, Steph. I got this."

"Oh, no you don't," I whispered. I hit the ground running on the other side of the fence, cutting through a dirty courtyard behind Mac's stand. The next low wall had someone's empty beer bottles lined up like shooting targets on the top, which clattered to the pavement as I went up and over. The smash of breaking glass sent an involuntary shiver over my skin. I resisted the urge to look back to see if Deacon had heard.

That was probably the only reason I saw the car before it hit me. The driver swerved, laying on the horn. I flattened up against the nearest wall and waved a half-hearted apology. If only more people viewed, "sorry, I'm running from the feds," as a viable excuse for doing stupid shit.

Once the car was gone, I listened for a moment. Hearing nothing, I darted down the street and zipped over yet another barricade, doubling back toward my original position. I'd thought I could maybe fake Deacon out by staying close by. Turns out I hadn't given him enough credit.

Gravity took over before I could reverse my movement, and I dropped down right in front of him. We stared at each other for a moment.

His radio crackled. "Well, you better hope she can set the record straight, Deacon. I don't have time to be chasing petty criminals around Brooklyn."

The voice was so steely, it had to belong to the woman I'd just seen with Deacon. My present situation was not ideal, but I thanked my lucky stars she hadn't followed me, too. Something told me she would've carted me off to jail in a heartbeat if I looked at her the wrong way.

"That's why you're going back to the office while I handle things out here. I'll update you when I get back."

"Fine. Good luck."

"Didn't know you had a partner," I remarked, leaning up against the fence, trying to look as casual as possible.

Deacon made a face that stopped within an inch of rolling his eyes. "I typically don't." He let out his breath. "The belief is that turning the investigation into a 'team assignment' will help ensure that progress gets made."

"And how's that working out for you?" I examined my nails, as if there was anything to look at. All I wanted was to seem bored instead of nervous.

"Well…" He drawled the word, his gaze a tangible

sensation on my face. "Got me a chance to get up close and personal with you again, so I'd call that a win."

"So that's your play. Use the same strategy as last time—a dash of flirtation to make the interrogation go down easy."

"There's no play—honest. I'm just here to talk."

"I've heard that line before."

He laughed. "All right, look. I'll level with you. The bureau is completely stumped. I can't figure out what the hell happened back at the slaughterhouse a couple weeks ago, and it's making me lose my beauty sleep." Running a hand over his finely coiffed hair, he grinned. "Not that you'd be able to tell."

That got a tiny smirk from me. "What makes you think I can help you with that? Last time we spoke face to face, I was in jail because someone else caused a disturbance at a comics convention. Not exactly the other side of the coin."

He arched his eyebrows. "Yeah, I looked into that, too. Your friend didn't just cause a disturbance, he pulled a damn sword. On a *celebrity*. You're lucky as hell Cruze started crying. That's the only reason he kept the whole incident quiet." I snorted a laugh, and Deacon continued. "Anyway, give me a little credit here, Vic. It took like five minutes to trace that place back to the mob. And another five to figure out that Rocco Durant's a missing man now. Puzzle pieces have a way of fitting together in the end."

"Don't talk like you caught me, man. I'm gonna need you to give me more than that."

"Okay." He began to tick a list off on his fingers. "How about video footage of you recovered from the scene? Audio of your voice? Eyewitness testimonials from at least five women who came forward and told us about being saved from a cage by a woman who matches your description?"

That is compelling, Marcus said.

Again, I barely managed not to jump, but Marcus was right. In the quiet aftermath of the slaughterhouse incident, I'd forgotten about all of Rocco's security measures. And I should have known that just because one girl chose a lawyer over the cops, that didn't mean the others would follow suit.

Deacon had led me into a trap. We both knew it. At a loss for non-incriminating words, I opted for stony silence, hoping he would break first. Surprisingly, he did.

"I don't want to take you in, Vic. Trust me. I'm fully aware that whatever your role was, I've got bigger fish to fry. But I think you might be able to help me or, at least, let me know where Rocco Durant is."

"You must be desperate if it's come to this. Back alley negotiations with your only lead."

"We are *not* negotiating." There was a hint of fire in his eyes now, a smolder that warned me not to poke too hard unless I wanted the flames to turn into a blaze.

I lifted my chin. "Aren't we?"

I'd never been able to resist the allure of danger.

For the second time, Deacon appeared to give up the chase. He slumped his shoulders, studying the ground. "I guess it doesn't matter. We've hit a wall. Either nobody knows shit, or they're just not talking to me." He scowled. "Experience tells me the second option is much more likely."

"Maybe you need to learn to ask nicely," I suggested.

"Yeah, yeah." His brooding eyes roved over our surroundings. "If it were up to me, I'd start bashing heads in tomorrow, but you can't do that when there's a badge involved. I've got rules to follow."

The admission was unexpectedly candid—and relatable. It also gave me an idea that I couldn't believe had eluded me for so long. All of a sudden, I was itching to slip away.

"Sucks to be you!" I made my voice as cheerful as possible. "In my line of work, we don't have those kinds of restrictions." While he wasn't looking at me, I took the opportunity to scan for possible escape routes behind him. From this side of the alley, it was obvious how he'd beat me at my own escape game.

Tables were about to turn, but first, I had to get behind him.

"Your line of work isn't work," he said pointedly. "I wish you'd give it up so I didn't have to come at you like an adversary. We had a good time at that party, didn't we?"

"That was before I knew about the badge in your pocket."

"You know, for someone who's been insisting she's done nothing wrong, you're not making a real strong case for innocence, Vic."

"Well, you're not making a real strong case for the FBI, Deacon." Deciding that the best option was just to be bold, I pushed myself up off the fence and strode past him. My shoulder brushed his rock-hard bicep.

"Words hurt." He reached out but missed my arm.

"Don't." I was walking backward now, making him

watch me get away. "What do they say in court? Beyond a reasonable doubt? Call me when that's what you've got."

"Hey." He moved to come after me, but his radio crackled. That same icy voice cut him off.

"Status report, Deacon. What the hell is taking you so long?"

Deacon's whole face hardened. He raised the receiver to his lips. "See you in a few, Steph."

Highly satisfied, I did a showy little pirouette and ran off in a very specific direction.

The next place wasn't very far away. And it was one I'd seen before.

Are we going where I think we are going?

"Yep." I muttered, in case Deacon was still within earshot. "Time to try an interrogation of our own."

6

FRANK WAS NOT where I'd assumed he would be, but for some reason, the guy tending the grimy bar didn't have any qualms about telling me where he thought Frank might have gone.

"Old rat bastard's probably at Dickey's. A few blocks from here. And he still has money on his tab, so feel free to shoot his nuts off when you see him."

A novel idea, Marcus murmured approvingly.

Not my original plan, but worth considering, depending on Frank's level of cooperation. I thanked the bartender and made a beeline for Dickey's. It didn't take long to see that it was a minor step up from the holes in the wall I was used to. For one thing, the lights in the barroom actually worked. For another, there was no brown haze of smoke oozing out the door—yes, even in our smoke-free city.

Looks like Frank is moving up in the world.

He stood out like a sore thumb, with his extra-wide

frame crammed onto a stool at the curve of the L-shaped bar. I would have recognized that slouch and that awful hair from a mile away. He'd been keeping his head down since Rocco's untimely disappearance, but as soon as I stepped into that place, I knew things hadn't changed that much for my favorite sleazebag.

Still, he was the one who'd tipped me off about the vampire factory in the first place, so I was inclined to play nice this time.

Or nicer than usual, anyway.

"Gimme a straight bourbon on the rocks." I signaled the bartender, sliding onto the stool next to Frank. He gave me a bleary glance, then did a double take.

"Aw, hell no. Not you again."

"What's the matter, Frank? I thought we were pals." My fingernails tapped restlessly on the polished surface of the bar. No doubt, he remembered what had happened last time we met. He needed to know it could always go that way again.

"Fuck off, girlie," he growled. "Everything went to shit, and I got a feeling it's your fault. Don't ask me how I know, but you ain't convincing me otherwise."

"Oh, please. Tell me more about your stunning intuition."

He grunted. "All's I know is, you came in asking where Rocco went and twisting my family jewels into a pretzel."

Marcus chortled. *I am sorry to have missed such a spectacle.*

"We talked some, yeah," I said, remembering it fondly.

"Uh huh." Frank grasped his glass in one huge paw and

took a swig. "And now he's nowhere to be found. Ain't gotta tell me that's no coincidence."

"I'm impressed by that logic, Frankie. Didn't know you had it in you." The barkeep put my drink down in front of me. I picked it up, testing the weight of the glass. It had a nice, heavy base, and I held it as I scooted even closer to Frank. "Now, I'm going to ask you for something, and if you don't give it to me, I'll make sure this glass ends up where the sun don't shine. And you'll be lucky if it's still in one piece when it gets there."

Briefly, his rough skin blanched underneath the rose tint of burgeoning intoxication. Then he smiled, which I didn't like. My instincts for trouble reared their head.

"Try me," he said. "You think I didn't learn my lesson? I ain't the smartest crayon in the box, but I'm no damn fool, neither. Frank don't go anywhere alone these days." The smile widened. A gold-capped tooth gleamed on the side of his mouth. "How about I introduce you to some of my friends. I'm sure they're just dying to meet ya."

I shoved away from him and sprang to my feet, abruptly aware of the hush that had fallen over the room. Every other set of eyes in that place was locked on me. Anticipation thickened the air.

"Where the hell did you get an army?" I demanded. None of them were vampires—that much was clear right away—and that meant none of them were too much of a threat.

Poor Frank didn't know that, but I let him have his moment.

"Outcasts." He spoke with a tinge of pride. "They didn't turn us into bloodsuckers, so we're out of the club, I guess.

Thing is, we're still loyal to our own rules. And I'm connected enough to know that we could make some serious coin bringing your head in on a plate. Ain't that right, boys?"

A ragged cheer went up from the ragtag crew. Most of them were like Frank, middle-aged, kind of tubby, clad in suits that probably fit ten years ago. I noticed, though, that they all had a fierce gleam in their eyes. There was a lot of anger in these downtrodden men, and it was about to come barreling straight at me.

I groaned. "Don't make me kill your bros, Frank. It's too early in the day."

"You? Ha!" He pounded the bar with a fist. "Lady, you might have tied my balls in a damn fisherman's knot, but if I had to bet on you or half this shitty bar, I'm putting my money on the bar."

With that, he signaled his pack.

They were slow, and I was ready. Holding the *Gladius Solis*'s hilt in one hand and brandishing a barstool in the other, I watched them ooze toward me in a sweaty tide. Some of them rolled up their sleeves as they lumbered, as if that would make a difference. When they got close enough, I chucked the stool into their ranks. It hit the first casualty squarely in the center of the forehead.

He went down like a sack of rocks. The guy right behind him lunged, his fist primed to connect with some part of me. Nonplussed, I grabbed the punch out of the air, twisting his thick wrist to the side. He yelped like a wounded dog.

You are being wasteful, Victoria. Every one of these men has a weakness that you are failing to exploit to its fullest potential.

"It's a bar fight, not an art installation." I struck a guy three times my size in his almost-nonexistent throat. He croaked, clutching at his Adam's apple. "You can put the critiques away."

Not if I want to make you into a halfway respectable warrior.

"I thought that was your deal." Someone grabbed me from behind with thick, muscled arms. I hooked my hands around his elbows and bent forward hard at the waist, tossing his considerable bulk into another advancing wave. They scattered like howling bowling pins.

Not long after that, the scene devolved into fat, flailing dominoes among a drunken herd of wildebeests. A bottle came sailing out of nowhere and struck me square on the head, showering me with little bits of glittery shrapnel.

"Son of a bitch!" I shouted, more out of annoyance than anything else. I could feel a thin trickle of blood along my temple, but the pain that should have gone with it was nowhere to be found.

Good, Marcus observed. *You have become sufficiently durable. The strength of Carcerum is with you from the nectar.*

I was pissed about the bottle, but damn if he wasn't right. A veritable hailstorm of flying appendages, and all I had to do was fend off the occasional fist or foot that made it close enough to my person. One more unlucky scumbag got heaved back into his comrades, under whom he promptly disappeared.

I wasn't planning on killing any of these idiots. They didn't *really* deserve it, and they weren't worth the effort. But I wasn't about to be gentle, either, and if they happened to get hurt in the process of trying to kill me? That was just collateral damage.

I pretended the bladeless hilt in my hand was a pistol and set to whipping, working my arm with the rhythm of a machine. Even the ones who were already down got conked in the side of the head. This little chat was between Frank and me. No witnesses.

Frank, for his part, stayed put on his stool as the drama unfolded around him, staring wide-eyed as his forces were demolished. He was shaking when I finished off his crew and returned to him, the beer glass dripping foam and ale onto the wood. The bartender was nowhere to be seen.

"What the hell?" he sputtered.

I shrugged. "Your help blows chunks, asshole. Maybe there's a reason you didn't get to play with the big boys in the first place."

Frank's chins quivered. "That was low."

The bourbon glass was back in my hand. "So, let me repeat myself. If you don't tell me what I want to know, you're gonna be shitting bourbon for a week." The sword hilt twirled lazily in my other hand. He eyed it from the corner of his vision. Beads of sweat stood out on the wide plane of his forehead.

He was still one hundred percent the Frank I knew—a big, lunkhead coward. Part of me loved him for it.

"This is bullshit," he said. "What the hell do you think I can tell you? Didn't you hear a thing I said? We're out. Finished. Cut off. Those dogshit vampires don't want nothing to do with us."

Interesting. I was unaware that survivors were permitted to exist outside of Delano or Lorcan's control. This could mean that there are other loopholes. These potential lapses in security must be duly punished.

I agreed, and I wanted Frank to get to the good stuff already. He was too busy moping into his drink to see me coming. I put the end of the sword hilt into his sternum and shoved. A thick wheeze squeezed itself from his chest, and in the next instant, he was sprawled on the ground.

"Dammit, why do you always gotta do this?" he spat, struggling to maintain his breath. "Do I look young to you? I can't live like this."

Gravity sank the hilt farther into his generous torso. He squirmed. I could tell he thought something extremely unpleasant was going to befall him at any moment. Little did he know, I couldn't do that to him. Frank was simply too much fun.

Time continues to flow, Victoria. Do not spend too much of it toying with hapless underlings.

He was right. I lifted the butt of the now-bladeless sword a little so that Frank had room to get a full breath in. The guy gulped the air like a drowning man.

"Now you're just being dramatic," I said.

He narrowed his baggy eyes at me. "You're a real card, you know that, honey? Look, all right." Grasping for the nearest stool, he used the leg to haul himself halfway to a sitting position. A few truly disgusting coughs rocked his torso. "Just lemme paddle back across the damn River Styx."

I poked the hilt into his belly and rolled my eyes. "Some of us don't have all day, Frank. You gonna talk, or do you want this up your ass? Cause I'm happy to oblige." The ice jangled against the walls of the glass. An expression of vague sickness crossed Frank's countenance.

"Jeezum Crow. Well, you're not going to believe me, but the mob's dead, sweet cheeks. At least, as far as I'm concerned. Some freaky shit went down a few weeks back, and everybody scattered to the damned winds. Like I said, I didn't take a deal with the devil, so I'm out of the loop. And you know what? That's fine by me. Means I don't need to risk my ass for these dickheads who don't give a shit about me."

His flabby face was redder than ever. After he stopped talking, he pounded the left side of his chest, and I wondered if his heart was about to burst. "Tell me what you heard, then. The rumor mill must be alive and well."

Frank grimaced. "Not the way it was before the vamps crashed the party. Only thing I know for sure is that there's a big job out west, and that's because it was set in motion before Rocco's plans went tits up. They never shared the details with us grunts, so I don't know them. Okay? That's it."

"Where out west?" I prodded him with the sword.

"Hell if I know. Somewhere in Cali is what I heard. Lot of guys been going out that way and never coming back, if you get my drift. Seems like they had the right idea."

If they are still alive, that is.

My thoughts exactly. "And you're absolutely sure you don't know specifics about this 'big job,' Frank? Because I have ways of finding stuff out, and if this all comes back to you in the end, you can bet you'll be seeing me again."

He gave me a bitter look. "Were your parents pitbulls,

kid? I told you all of it. Maybe this time, you'll leave me alone for a whole month."

"If you're lucky." But before I left, I helped Frank to his feet, pulling on one corpulent arm until he stood unsteadily with his hands on the counter. "Here. This drink's on me." I left the glass in front of him.

He muttered something indistinct as I left. "Did you hear what he said?" I asked Marcus.

I believe it was, 'Thanks.'

I smiled. "See, he's learning some manners. I'm already making life better down here."

7

THE NEXT MORNING, I paced through my training with a million other thoughts zooming around my brain. The dissolution of the mob meant that Frank hadn't been quite as rich a resource as I'd hoped. There were still vast gaps in my understanding of what was going on behind the scenes, but if this mystery job out west was big enough to move bodies three thousand miles, then it was definitely something to look into.

But where could I dig up more information? I hated the feeling of flying blind and flying mostly blind wasn't much better.

"What do you think, Marcus?" I asked. "We've seen Deacon, and we just saw Frank. Jules needs to stay all the way in the dark, so that means I'm out of people. You're up."

During my service to Kronin, he would frequently send me to deal with rogue Forgotten elements. Oftentimes I was sent in relatively blind.

"So what did you do?"

It was simple, really. Just search out the bizarre, the strange, the out of place. The Forgotten have a way of disrupting the natural order of things. The gods leave their fingerprints on everything.

"Well the tabloids have turned up squat, and we don't exactly have an eyes on view of the world here in my shitty apartment." I thought for a second, then the answer hit me like a metric ton of bricks. "Marcus, I know exactly where we need to look. The greatest compendium of the bizarre the world has ever known."

What is it? An oracle of some kind? An academy of the philosophers?

"Even better. It's called the internet."

This net, it will help us find what we need?

"Trust me—if you were impressed by the newspaper, the internet is going to blow your medallion-trapped mind. But I don't exactly have a computer on hand. We'll have to head down to the library."

There were truly astonishing libraries in my lifetime, Marcus remarked, almost dreamily. *They contained tomes of knowledge in multitudes, stacked higher than a man could climb. Given sufficient time, one could obtain all the secrets of the world and beyond, if he so desired.*

"Right, right. We totally still have that." I had neither the heart nor the patience to attempt to explain the slow, inexorable advance of digitization. He'd see it for himself when we got there.

I sped up my sword strikes, channeling all my replenished energy into the downstrokes. The actual hilt was my weapon this session; the training swords had begun to look more like oversized toothpicks. It was a weird exercise of will to keep my mind from summoning the golden blade. There was little doubt that it could easily start a fire in the loft or cleave through the floor.

But soon, I wasn't even thinking about the blade anymore. "We'll head to the library," I announced. "As soon as I'm done with this."

How is that possible? Those locations must be ancient in this time.

"No, no. These ones are modern, but the concept is the same. You'll see."

Finishing my routine in a hurry, I put the sword aside, grabbed my bar of soap, and took a shower by dumping a bucket of lukewarm water over my head as I stood in the middle of the non-functional tub. The suds threatened to run down into my eyes as I scrubbed my scalp clean and wished for the umpteenth time that the meager plumbing in my loft extended to a proper shower.

Not that I wasn't grateful for a working toilet—I was, immensely. But a true hot shower was one of the comforts I missed the most. It was moments like that one, me standing behind a wall of cardboard and washing my hair out of a bucket, that I realized with the most clarity how abnormal everything had become.

And maybe, just fleetingly, I let myself get close to wanting normalcy again.

The feeling didn't stay. I finished rinsing, pulled some clothes on, kicked myself into high gear for the day. My hastily combed hair was still damp as I ran down the steps of my building out into the street. When was the last time

I'd felt this kind of excitement over paying a visit to a public institution?

It was almost exhilarating in a super nerdy kind of way. This must have been how Marcus felt all the damn time.

When I was a soldier, there existed a library that was the pinnacle of its kind in Alexandria. His voice took on a wistful timbre. *I was there once, in my younger years. Never again did I lay my eyes on such utter grandeur, until I reached Carcerum. The wisdom in that place was palpable.*

"I went to the public library on a field trip in middle school," I told him. "Spent most of the time frenching Tommy Minksi behind the stacks. But I do remember them teaching us how to use computers to do research."

What is 'frenching?' A form of warfare that you did on these 'computers?'

I barked out a short laugh. "There's an answer to that question, my friend, but I don't have time for it." I shook my head. "I might never have time for *that* one." Trying to imagine explaining modern romance or the internet to Marcus made my head spin.

He'd see one of the two in action soon enough.

We went to the branch on Fifth Avenue where I thought the immediate resource pool would be largest. A library card was something I hadn't even thought of in years, and I had no intention of borrowing anything long term. With my recent luck, it would be lost or torn to shreds within a day.

"Ready?" I scaled the steps leading up to the central doors and laid my hand on the wood.

A champion is always ready, Victoria.

I pushed open the doors. The unmistakable scent of

print and paper washed over me. I took a deep breath in. It reminded me of the back office in my parents' shop, and so did the ambient sounds of patrons checking out books and returning them, pages shuffling gently in that peculiar library stillness. For a split second, I was a kid again, tucked into the cubbyhole in my dad's desk, listening to him keep the books.

This is not a library, Marcus said.

"Just you wait." I went past the circulation desk, up some more stairs, and across the threshold into the first book chamber. "How about now?"

My stars. The wonder ran deep in his words, obviously evoking memories of his own. *It is not Alexandria, but the feeling. The feeling is the same. Would that I had lived long enough to experience this place in my own body.*

"That's what you've got me for." What I didn't tell him was that I wasn't here for the books. I passed the towering stacks, the long study tables, and the glass-walled cubicles for librarians and research assistants.

Where are you going? Surely, there must be something in this vast chamber that could be of use to us.

"Maybe. But it would take way too long to find it. So, we're heading toward the future instead." A sign reading "Digital Media Center" adorned a doorway at the end of the room.

Bingo.

I do not understand. Marcus sounded legitimately disappointed, and I felt a little bad. Maybe once all this was over, I'd come back and get a library card after all, just to make it up to him. For now, he'd have to deal with the fast lane.

I paused in the entrance to the digital media center. "It's

like this." To my left were the looming rows of books. "All this stuff is the past." I gestured to the right, at corresponding rows of computers, printers, copiers, and all kinds of other stuff Marcus couldn't hope to fathom. "This is the future. And if we're looking for something out of the ordinary, this will be our best bet."

Illuminate me, he said.

There was one free computer in the very back, which I snagged before anyone else could. It made me feel better to sit with my back to the wall, especially given the sensitive nature of my research. It seemed unlikely that a standard search engine would unearth secrets of the gods, but the internet was full of surprises.

"Watch this," I said to Marcus.

Following my conversation with Frank, I was fairly certain Lorcan was at work on the west coast. But that didn't exactly narrow things down. I took a wild stab. My first search, *jobs in California,* brought up mostly employment sites in an abundance of fields. I went five pages deep into the results before I gave up. Then I tried *news in California,* in case strange things were plaguing the west coast the same way they'd begun to plague New York.

No luck.

I am unconvinced by this technology, Vic. We had more success with your newspapers.

"Ugh. Just give me a second." I sat back in the chair, tapping my chin to encourage thought. The third time, I typed, *events in California.* At first, this one looked like a bust as well. Halfway down the first page, a link caught my eye. "'A LIGHT in the Cosmos'; Keynote Speaker Silas Monk. Silicon Valley Global Tech Expo, Palo Alto, California?" The words struck a weird chord of familiarity in my memory, so strongly that I actually shut my eyes to try and recall whatever it was. Imagine my surprise when the slack-jawed, gap-toothed mug of that shitty vamp in the alleyway floated to the top of my brain. His voice echoed distantly.

"Pretty soon, we're gonna have a light of our own."

"Whoa," I muttered. Could that possibly be a coincidence? Didn't seem likely.

None of those terms are familiar to me, said Marcus, yanking me back to the headline on the blog

I ignored him and clicked on the link. It brought me through to a sleek, simplistic blog post discussing the finer points of the Expo, including dates, times, and special guests. "Hey, Marcus, this is next week!" A thought blossomed in my head. "What if the reason those mobsters weren't coming back is that they've been sent to get ready for this thing?"

Why would the mobbing ones be so invested? Delano and Lorcan both have power that far surpasses the capacity of humans. They have no need for your technology.

"Maybe, but I think you're wrong on this one. Back in your era, human technology might have carried no more damage potential than sticks and stones, but these days, we've got enough power in the US alone to blow the world up a hundred times over. You said Lorcan was a master of using everything at his disposal to his advantage. This could be it."

I scrolled quickly, skimming the text. The guest list had two names on it. The first, Silas Monk, I recognized. Inventor, innovator, and technological guru, he had fast become the darling of the internet age. It stood to reason that he'd be attending any Global Tech Expo.

"It says he's going to be revealing some new advancement he's been developing. But there's nothing about what kind of tech it is." I hit the back button and scoured the following search results for something more. Just below the Global Tech Expo blog was a post entitled, "The Monsters in Silas Monk's Closet."

Modern technology wasn't exactly in my wheelhouse, but I knew a thing or two about monsters.

"Check this out." The post's original location was a blog called Valley of Shadows. All of the site's content was maintained and curated by someone named SplitScreen. What intrigued me the most was its sheer volume. Split-Screen had gathered pages and pages of lengthy articles on the noted inventor, and not just regular interviews or biographical stuff, either.

I had stumbled on a treasure trove of what looked like conspiracy theories. On closer inspection, however, some of the details didn't seem so far-fetched. Not in the world I knew.

Who is this SplitScreen? Marcus asked.

"Beats me. But they're presenting meticulously researched evidence that in addition to coming up with cool apps, Monk works on weapons' contracts for the government. Most of this info is redacted, but I don't know. I can't say it's fake." The documents, both digital and scanned, certainly looked real enough to my untrained eye. If it was a hoax, it was a damn good one. "And holy shit." I inhaled sharply and received a nasty look from a mean spirited librarian.

Lowering my voice, I leaned in closer to the screen.

"Look here. This blog says here that several employees of Monk Industries have been murdered in the last few months. Their bodies were found exsanguinated. Apparently, local law enforcement has kept the whole thing under wraps."

I pushed back from the keyboard and rubbed my eyes.

That sounds like Lorcan's minions at play. We must go quickly before they have more time to spread their sinister network. How long will it take to journey to this California?

"Six hours, give or take." I navigated to the contact page on SplitScreen's blog. A lone email address stood out against the white background, betraying no hints as to its owner's identity. I copied it down. Maybe they knew more about Monk than they had put online.

"Okay, Marcus. I've got one question for you."

Yes?

"You ever seen an airplane before?"

8

THE WALLET I carried onto the plane at JFK, and then off again at SFO, was entirely my own. I'd been way too absorbed in the massive trip I was about to undertake to spare a thought toward pilfering from anyone. The cost of my plane ticket barely even registered to me. I still had a credit card left over from better days that I saved for special occasions only, on account of hardly ever being able to pay it off.

This was as special as things were going to get.

And hell, if the world were coming to an end at the hands of the gods, the last thing I really needed to worry about was my credit score.

So, having procured my passage one hundred percent honestly, I felt no shame as I settled into my window seat near the middle of the plane. It was a nonstop flight, and I planned to sleep for most of the six hours and ten minutes. Marcus, however, was too gobsmacked by the whole idea of flight to be chill.

I should have known.

What is this contraption? He asked this while I gazed out of my window across the long wing of the jet. *It's like sitting in the galley of a ship. But there is no water. How is it going to get us to California?*

"It flies, dude." I spoke very, very softly so that my seat-mate wouldn't hear me talking to myself. "Like we're about to go six miles up into the sky and not come down until we're on the other side of the country. Bet that's a sentence you never thought you'd hear."

Marcus didn't believe me until it happened. Then, I was forced to take off the medallion and put it into the seat back pocket in front of me. I had no idea a spirit could yell so damn loud.

We got off in San Francisco just as the sun was beginning to slide behind a bank of clouds in the western half of the sky. Renting a car to drive the thirty-four miles to Palo Alto had been a consideration, but a cursory search of average hotel rates told me to find a room in the city and brave the commute. I told myself I'd fit in better that way: another young, eager techie driving into the IT Valhalla that was Silicon Valley.

But who was I kidding? Pretty much anyone could tell by glancing in my general direction that I did not belong in the polished, freakishly utopian world of the technological elite. Everywhere I looked, I saw people integrated with machines in one way or another. Glasses with glowing frames that augmented the wearer's reality. Unmanned, remote-controlled delivery drones laden with small pack-ages, whirring casually through the air. At the first crosswalk, I noticed that not all of the cars at the light had drivers behind their steering wheels.

You know, totally normal shit.

This is inconceivable. I had no idea humans were capable of such rapid progression.

Honestly, neither did I. Maybe it was the five years spent basically living under a rock, but being at the cutting edge like this was sort of stunning. It made me wonder if New York had a similar gleaming allure under all the layers of filth.

Nah, probably not.

I dug my phone out of my bag and thumbed the email app. Right before we left New York behind, I had sent SplitScreen the blogger a little message. Nothing too drastic or unfriendly; just a heads-up that I knew of yet another juicy secret Silas Monk was hiding.

Mostly it was another stab in the dark. Who knew what a face-to-face with a tech blogger would get me? It had taken me over an hour to comb through the blogger's posts and links on Monk, and I couldn't imagine that there wasn't more inside of their head about the tech mogul. Maybe my charm could elicit a bit more useful data. At this point, anything might help.

For six hours, there had been no response, but something popped up as I trotted across the street in the middle of a jostling crowd.

It was an email from SplitScreen.

Tomorrow. 11 AM. Adam's Rib. Back left corner table. Come alone.

"Yes!" Part of me couldn't believe they responded. "Did you see that, Marcus? Tomorrow! I can't wait to find out who this really is." Or what sort of dirt they could help me dig up. Maybe Monk had a secret identity. Maybe Monk *was* the secret identity. Maybe there was a whole other dimension to things that I had so far completely missed.

I shouldn't have been hoping for that last one, but hey, knowledge was power, right? And I really needed to know if Monk was Lorcan's target, or if he was a key player in the game. The last thing I wanted to do was travel three thousand miles just to spin my wheels in different scenery.

After days of chasing down wild geese, it finally seemed as though we were about to get somewhere for real.

Victoria, I have a concern.

"What's up?" A big grin spread across my face. Not even Marcus's tendency to act like a stick in the mud could bring me down from this high.

As far as I am aware, you do not actually possess any new information regarding Monk or his ideas. No doubt, this person intends to question you thoroughly about the nature of your intelligence. What do you plan to say?

"I dunno." I shrugged. "I'll make something up. If I do it well enough, it'll get them to say something big." All I needed was confirmation that Silas Monk was a lead worth pursuing. What did that sound like? I wasn't sure. But I was confident I'd know it when I heard it.

Marcus was silent, thoughtful. *And you believe this to be an effective strategy?*

"Why not? I've talked my way out from under the mob plenty of times before. It's gonna be fine, man. I know what I'm doing."

If you say so, Victoria. Although your past record does not grant a positive outlook on the future.

I couldn't help but smile. "Bite me, Centurion."

Marcus could be a Debbie Downer all he wanted—that was his problem, not mine. Now that SplitScreen was in the bag, I had two more things to do.

One: find a room.

And two: figure out how the hell we were going to speak to Silas Monk. Sure, my hopes were high for the meeting tomorrow, but not even I was naïve enough to trust a conspiracy theorist blogger to give up everything they knew. Ultimately, we'd have to get to Monk.

I had a feeling he wasn't going to be as accessible as Cameron Cruze. And I sure as hell couldn't barge into the Expo with my sword out.

Greater men than I had already tried that and failed.

The first thing I saw about the west coast, other than its techno-fantasyland image, was that it was expensive as shit to stay anywhere. Fortunately, available resources appeared to match the cost of survival, as long as you had a particular skill set. The downside?

Those skills were starting to seem a little too aggressively immoral, what with Marcus talking nonstop about honor and heroism right in my head. I won't lie and say I didn't think about trying to filch from one of the overly polished dickwads strutting down the street, but I just couldn't bring myself to do it. Checking my reserve, I saw I had enough to get by for at least a few days, provided I lived on a pretty tight budget.

Good thing I was no stranger to that. But I'd have to find a way to remedy my finances eventually.

In a city like this one, money always talked.

The place I chose was a little motel, the kind where the

doors faced out toward the parking lot and headlights shined through your windows at night. Far more glamorous digs surrounded the spot, but no respectable establishment would take cash only. A nice place would ask questions, and I didn't want to push my luck. No one would be there to post bail for me in San Francisco.

The cash I had on hand bought me three nights to start, one of which I was about to spend. Seeing that the check-in slip asked for the make, model, and license plate of my car, I was suddenly glad I hadn't rented one yet. I still needed to, but now, the motel didn't have to know about it.

Score one stealth point for Vic.

I felt pretty good on my way to the room, key jingling merrily on its chain. "What do you think, Marcus? What's Lorcan up to?

It is hard to say. He was powerful enough to deceive even Kronin, which means his moves will be far from predictable. But in New York, he sent his agent Delano to infiltrate positions of influence. It's possible he will do more of the same here.

"Monk is influential all right, but I have a hard time picturing him as a particularly potent vampire. The bigger question is, what would Lorcan want Monk's influence for?" I switched the television to a local news channel and flopped back against the plumped-up pillows. "Man, this bed feels amazing."

That is indeed the question.

A news anchor's smooth voice filtered in one ear and out the other. A car accident on the freeway, an increased risk of brush fires due to recent drought, a measure going forward to mitigate the extent of smog pollution above the city. Zero mentions of exsanguinated corpses leading back to Silas Monk.

That didn't mean squat. The guy was more than powerful enough to smother undesirable press. No, the bottom of this was way, way down. Near the center of the Earth, maybe.

"Well then let's just ask him. He's in town for the Expo, so this could be our best bet to grab a little chat. I wonder how hard it would be to locate where he's staying."

Likely not in an abandoned slaughterhouse.

"And thank goodness for that."

I punched Monk's name into the search bar on my phone. On the outside, the venerated tech mogul looked like an average guy surrounded by amazing things.

"He looks like he could be a math teacher," I remarked. "A math teacher with seven luxury cars."

Was it as simple as that? Money could go a long way to establishing an army. Maybe Monk was the prime investor bankrolling whatever was in the works behind the gods' invisible curtain? It certainly seemed possible—the guy looked rich enough to buy whole continents.

Which raised a whole new set of questions. What was he funding and why?

9

ANTICIPATION CUT through my efforts to sleep that night, despite the major bed upgrade and the forty-minute hot shower. Lying on my side in the dark, I ran through all the possibilities I could think of as to who SplitScreen might be.

A random blogger? Or just a whackjob conspiracy theorist?

Or maybe a bigwig at Monk Industries who had too much at stake to use their real name?

I rolled onto my back and slipped the medallion around my neck. "Hey, Marcus?"

Hail, Victoria. What bothers you at this early hour?

"How big do you think this is? Like how deep does the rabbit hole go here?"

Are you asking me what level of trouble you may find yourself in, should you see this through to the end?

I smirked. "Yeah, more or less."

Marcus took his time to reply. Then he said, *It is trouble of the highest order. A deep and roiling ocean. There are hidden depths and currents you cannot hope to see until you are already drowning. But I will do my best to guide you and keep you afloat, even through the worst of times. We shall not be defeated.*

The smirk on my lips softened into a real smile. I closed my eyes. "You got that right. These techheads won't know what hit 'em."

He was quiet for a while. Then he said, *It is possible that this place has become entrenched in the gods' dealings while we were busy cleaning up after Lorcan in New York. Promise me that you will be careful.*

"Yeah, of course." I stifled a yawn. It figured that as soon as he started getting serious, my sleep drive would start to kick in. "I'm like an old pro at this, remember?"

You are a young professional at best. At worst, you are simply young.

"That's why I got an old guy like you to help me out." I rolled onto my side and closed my eyes. "You just said it yourself, man. We're not going to let this beat us. All we have to do is meet up with this SplitScreen guy and find out what he knows. I've done this a million times before."

Are you comparing this person to one of your mob men back home?

"They're called mobsters," I said, grinning into the pillow. "And if SplitScreen is anything like Frank, then this is going to be a piece of cake. Trust me."

I trust you implicitly. But I do not trust others, and it is the others who hold the power at the moment.

"That's why we're here." I was mumbling now, sliding inevitably down toward sleep. "To get it back."

THE BIG PLATE glass window on the front of Adam's Rib, a little bistro wedged precariously on one of San Francisco's slanting side streets, both surprised and worried me. I hesitated on the approach, trying to see inside at an angle without looking too conspicuous. Doing this, I understood why my enigmatic contact had chosen it—peering inside proved to be difficult.

"Guess we're going in blind," I said to Marcus.

Do you know any other way?

A little bell chimed sweetly as I stepped across the threshold and into the presence of an empty reception counter. The sign standing nearby read: PLEASE SEAT YOURSELF. Following SplitScreen's instructions, I took the table in the back-left corner, just out of the window's range. It was then that I noticed the place was almost empty.

The hair on the back of my neck stood up, last night's confidence ebbing away. Was this a set-up?

As if on cue, Marcus murmured, *I do not like this.*

"That makes two of us. I feel like I'm about to be ambushed."

"Hi, welcome to Adam's Rib!" said a cheery voice angling in from over my shoulder. I looked up into the sparkling blue eyes of a waitress with a wide smile. Not the ambush I was expecting. "Are you waiting for someone?"

"Yes." My throat felt very dry. "Could I get a water, please?"

The longer I sat there, the more my brain screamed at

me to get the hell out, SplitScreen or no SplitScreen. I couldn't shake the feeling that I was being tricked.

Or that I was being watched.

"Of course," the waitress said. "Here, I'll leave you a menu to browse while you wait."

"Thanks." She walked away, and I turned my attention back to the giant window. Why did it make me so damn nervous? And where was SplitScreen? Only two other people occupied the restaurant besides me, and they were ensconced in their own little corner. A terrible thought occurred to me. "Marcus," I whispered. "What if this place is a front?"

What do you mean?

"I mean, what if it's not really a restaurant? I could've walked straight into a Trojan Horse just now."

Traditionally, the Trojan Horse did the walking.

"I'm not asking for a damn history lesson. I'm saying that I think we're in danger."

Probably, but it is too late to retreat now. You must be vigilant. Do not let anyone surprise you.

"Including the waitress?"

Especially the waitress.

Right on cue, she approached with a glass of water. I made a concentrated effort to wipe all hints of suspicion off my face.

"Here you are!" She just could not stop beaming directly into my eyeballs. "I'll give you a few minutes, okay?"

She thought I was being stood up. "Sure," I said. "Thank you."

Where the *hell* was SplitScreen?

Two more minutes ticked by in slow motion. I checked

my phone once for emails, then twice. On the third pass, Marcus gave me an auditory nudge. *Victoria. Observe.*

On the other side of the window, a small hooded figure came up to the door. The bell chimed. Their eyes were obscured by a giant pair of aviators, but the direction of their face made it look like they focused on my table. They made a beeline for me.

I kept my mouth shut until the stranger had slipped into the booth across from me. They'd pulled a hat down over the glasses, and the whole lower half of their face was obscured by a thick black scarf. We stared at each other.

"Tell me what you know," SplitScreen said.

I blinked.

SplitScreen was a girl.

She was also absolutely stone-faced, and the rainbowed reflective lenses of her aviators acted as an impenetrable defense against me. I'd expected her to unwrap the scarf from her face, but that was apparently not happening anytime soon. Her hands stayed under the table, out of sight. It made me nervous.

Was this chick packing heat?

"Spit it out," she said. "You said you had something good."

The touch of impatience jolted me back into real time. To my dismay, making something up was a lot harder with those damn aviators boring into my skull.

I would strongly advise you to not mention the gods at this juncture.

So naturally, my brain took the other path. "Monk is working with vampires."

That is not exactly what I meant.

"Keep your voice down," SplitScreen murmured. "Also, Vampires? What the *hell* are you talking about?"

Her head was turned just to the side, presumably so she could monitor the view out the front of the restaurant. Over her other shoulder, the smiling waitress angled back toward the table, but as soon as she saw my new companion, she made a neat U-turn.

I would have spent more time questioning it if I wasn't so relieved.

"Look, I saw your blog about the bodies," I said.

"There are a lot of those."

I pursed my lips. "The ones without blood in them."

"Uh huh. And your groundbreaking conclusion is vampires? *Twilight* much? I think I'm going to have to pass on this." She scooted her chair backward. "Thanks anyway, I guess. And if anyone asks, which they shouldn't, you never saw me, and you don't know who I am."

"No, wait." Desperation threatened to weave its way into my voice. "That's not the whole story. It's way bigger than that. I need your help."

She paused for a moment, on her feet. I could see her mulling it over, the gears turning behind her full-face getup. "You need *someone's* help. But probably not mine."

Then she pushed the chair in and strode toward the door before I had the chance to say anything else. I stood up, too, but it was too late. SplitScreen was out the door.

Hmm.

"Shut up. Don't you say a damn word." Watching her bundled form hurry toward the crosswalk, I sighed into my water. "Now what?"

I have received strict instructions not to say a word.

"Ugh. Marcus—"

As I stood their talking to thin air, a dark van swooped up to the curb, barely stopping as the side door slid open. One second, SplitScreen was there, and the next, she was gone in a cloud of exhaust.

"Holy shit! Did you see that?" It had not been my original intention to follow the blogger—even I had enough common sense to know that was a bad idea—but unless I'd hallucinated the last fifteen seconds, I had just witnessed her kidnapping.

And that changed things somewhat.

"Come on." I was talking to Marcus, even though he really had no choice in the matter. "We're going after her. This can't be a coincidence."

Go quickly. The nectar in your veins is not enough for you to outrun a steel chariot.

"It's enough for me to try." I brushed past the poor waitress on my way out, nearly spinning her around. "Sorry! I'm sorry. I just really have to go."

She called after me. "Thanks for stopping in!"

I reached the sidewalk just in time to catch the boxy back end of the van whipping left at the end of the block. The light at the intersection turned yellow, then red, and I took the opportunity to dart into the flow of traffic, zig-zagging around cars as they slowed to a stop. A chorus of half-angry, half-bewildered honks tracked my progress across the street, but as a native New Yorker, the noise barely registered in my consciousness.

I popped up over the opposite curb and dashed headlong after the retreating van. "Hey, can you read that plate for me?" I asked Marcus. "You're sort of all-knowing now, right?"

He frowned audibly. *As I've said before, my access to the world is currently limited to what your senses can provide. And your vision is far from perfect. I think we need a pair of correctional lenses.*

"Oh, that is bullshit!" But instead of wasting time and breath arguing with him, I pushed my legs harder. Another main street crossed up ahead, and this one was even more clogged with traffic. Not only that, but I spotted a narrow back way, which I knew from experience likely led to shortcuts.

While the van nudged its way into the crawling stream of cars and trucks, I zipped back across the asphalt and down the alley. Narrow urban spaces were quickly becoming my new native habitat. I guessed there were some things every city in the world must have in common.

At least this one didn't reek of garbage.

10

I SCRAMBLED over the dead-end wall and hit the ground running on the other side, keeping the main street city traffic on my left. The area beyond the alleyway turned out to be residential, dotted with fences, lots, and the occasional hedge. When I finally found access to the roadway again, at first, I couldn't see the van anywhere.

"Damn it to hell! I think—"

Over there.

The roof of the van drifted in the middle lane, twenty feet away. It was trying to carve a path, but midday traffic in San Francisco was just as unforgiving as its East coast counterpart. But, of course, as soon as I laid eyes on my target, the current picked up again. I needed to find a way to game the system and fast.

That was when I noticed the pedestrian bridge crossing over the street. "Aha!"

It was behind me in the wrong direction, but if I played my cards right, I could totally make up the difference. Or I hoped I could. Out of time, I sped toward the stairs, taking them two or three at a time. Although it wasn't a warm day, the sun beat down on the top of my head, and I felt weirdly exposed. A stiff breeze pulled its fingers through my hair.

I positioned myself over the correct side of the bridge and gazed down at the traffic passing below. The height hadn't looked like much on the ground, back when this had seemed like a good idea, but I felt the reliable old lurch in my stomach. Was I really about to fling myself off a city bridge just to try and catch up with a getaway van?

Yep.

The railing, made of strong metal piping, held my weight nicely. I perched on the rungs long enough to scout my landing prospects and get a feel for the black van's most likely route. There was an on-ramp in the near distance. It was probably heading for the freeway, which meant I had to get to it first or else I'd lose my mark for sure.

I stepped up higher on the railing, swaying in the breeze, eyes narrowed against the unrelenting sunshine. Directly below, a flatbed carrying what looked like a dumpster emerged from the shadow below the bridge. It was full of all kinds of weird garbage, but the thing I cared about the most was a slab of old foam resting across the top.

"Look at that," I said to Marcus. "It's like the universe wants me to do this kind of stupid shit."

I would tell you not to, but I know it will do no good, he responded. *Instead, I will request that you please attempt to preserve yourself. It would be an apocalyptic disaster if I had to find another hero, particularly in my current form.*

"No promises," I shouted, then lunged.

I pushed off the bridge with my back foot, catapulting into the air and crossing my fingers that I'd calculated correctly. The colored gleam of traffic fell away and then came rushing up to meet me way too fast. It was stupid, but I shut my eyes at the last second. If idiocy was going to wipe me off the planet, I didn't want to see it coming.

Instead of asphalt, my face struck the rough foam with all the grace of a botched Olympic dive. The edge of my molars dug into the inside of my cheek until I tasted blood, and the shock of impact reverberated through my whole skeleton, but when I rolled over and snapped my eyelids open, the cerulean blue of the sky beamed down at me. Moments later, the familiar scent of trash assaulted my nostrils. "San Francisco smells like ass."

Surely, you did not think this cushion rested atop a bed of flowers.

"Ugh." Gripping the edge of the shipping container, I pulled myself up on the rim and sat with my legs dangling over the hitch, peering over the roof of the cab for signs of the van. As expected, it signaled right and slid onto the freeway ramp almost as soon as I'd found it again. This time, luck was on my side. My driver followed suit.

I let out a sigh of relief. One crazy jump I could manage, but trying to switch rides would've been a total nightmare.

I wasn't sure how long I sat on that rectangle of foam, hunched over to protect myself from the wind. Every now and then, I poked my head up to make sure we were still tailing the van, and as soon as I saw it veering down the exit in front of us, I knew it was almost time to bail.

"Marcus?"

Yes?

"Full disclosure: I don't really know how to do this part."

You are about to find out. It's like all great adventures. Did I ever tell you about the time I battled a Griffin?

"Not now, Marcus," I shouted.

Making sure my grip was as tight as possible on the side of the container, I leaned down to try and get an idea of how fast we were actually moving. A loose strand of hair whipped into my face, bringing with it a sour stench. I grimaced. Maybe we weren't rocketing along at highway speeds anymore, but it still felt way too dangerous just to drop off the side.

Then the truck took a curve, and my center of gravity swung down, nearly solving the problem for me.

Victoria!

"Oh, shit! Shit!"

The force generated by the turning truck swung me dizzyingly outward before it crushed me up against the metal siding of the dumpster. My arm twisted, and a sharp, hot pain shot down from my shoulder. The adrenaline coursed through my veins, and I swear time stretched out for an instant or two.

The truck began to slow down, and its body straightened up, leaving me hanging like a damn windsock from the edge. I started to pull myself back up one-handed. Then, I saw a red traffic light coming up and embraced the lightning bolt of luck that had just been bestowed upon me. As the truck rumbled to a halt, I dropped ten feet to solid ground.

"That was way too fucking close," I muttered, darting off to the curb. Some car behind me emitted a confused little honk, but I didn't even look. I'd lived in a major metropolitan center long enough to know that eventually they'd see something weirder than a girl jumping out of a dumpster on a flatbed.

Are you all right?

"I'm great. It's not every day that I get to make a truck full of garbage look that cool." More importantly, I'd caught a glimpse of the black van on the other side of the intersection, making a right. "I mean, I don't smell as cool as I look, but don't worry about it. We need to move."

If I hadn't been sure about having heightened abilities before, booking it down that stretch of road made the transformation abundantly clear. Marcus was right—I couldn't quite keep pace with the van, but it wasn't shaking me off, either. I might have even gained some ground.

It felt pretty damn amazing. Not quite up to leaping a building in a single bound but amazing nonetheless. For the first time in years, there was a sense that things were getting better. In some ways, anyway.

After I saw where the van was headed, I understood that in other ways, things were about to get much, much worse.

The warehouse lot was poorly maintained, an uneven pit of rocky debris and loose gravel that sprayed from underneath the van's tires as it pulled into a space. I hung back under cover of the tall, scratchy grass along the side of the street, observing the panel door slide open again.

One guy lumbered out with SplitScreen practically tucked under his arm. Her obvious squirming didn't seem to slow him down one bit.

He joined up with the driver at the back and walked into the building with SplitScreen slung between them. I could see her thrashing, but again, her efforts were spectacularly ineffective.

She kind of reminded me of myself in the early days, except I didn't have anyone jumping into a heap of garbage to rescue me.

I cased the van with as much as a two-second sideways glimpse would let me while I tiptoed up to the warehouse door. Leaving it uninspected made me itch. That vehicle *had* to be a goldmine of information, but the blogger's safety took precedence over all of that.

After all, she was the one who could talk.

The only thing I saw with any clarity was a weird strip of white running down the body of the vehicle. The telltale sign of a careless sideswipe. So, these guys were shitty drivers, too. Maybe SplitScreen was lucky she'd made it this far in one piece.

I doubted she would agree with me on that one.

The door was solid and *very* locked. Soundproof, too, judging by its apparent weight and thickness. A rock began to form in the pit of my stomach. None of these signs were good. I hadn't forgotten what I'd found in the last large abandoned structure I broke into.

And I kept thinking about SplitScreen's story about those exsanguinated bodies.

"How long does it take to set up a vampire factory?" I

whispered to Marcus, sidling along the edge of the wall. "Could there be a new one in two or three weeks?"

If the benefactor is powerful enough, supplying the initial blood source would be a trivial matter. So, yes. Far too easily.

"Great." I felt for the shape of the sword hilt in my bag. "Maybe the cage will be full of grizzly bears this time."

The side of my foot struck something hard. I glanced down at a stack of cinder blocks, then up at the window just above them. "Don't tell me I'm not the first one to bust in here."

I suspect you will be the first to remain undetected.

The back of my neck prickled. I hoisted myself up onto the blocks and stood on my toes to peer in through the dirty pane. Unlike the New York location, this place was only one big, barren room. Naked lightbulbs hung on wires from the exposed beams in the ceiling. Whenever they were jostled by doors opening or heavy footsteps approaching, all the light jumped up along the walls.

I shivered. "Man, that's creepy." A few chairs and a battered table furnished the space. Suspicious stains dotted the floor.

I didn't see a pit or anything that looked like it might be concealing a pit.

I do not believe this to be a vampire creation facility, Marcus declared.

"Why doesn't that make me feel any better?"

Because it means we do not know who or what is using this place—and why.

At that moment, SplitScreen and her two escorts came into my field of vision. I shut my mouth, directing all my focus into sight and hearing. The guards shoved their captive into a chair. One started to secure her with some kind of cable. The other ripped the scarf and glasses from her face.

SplitScreen said something clearly nasty, and the goon hesitated, half a step from hitting her. Thinking better of it, he got out a roll of duct tape and taped her mouth shut instead. Her death glare transcended the distance and the grimy glass.

It made me want to be her friend—or, failing that, at least not her enemy.

The windowsill vibrated under my hand, a sensation I recognized from living in a half-condemned loft, indicating that a door had been opened somewhere. Sure enough, both burly guards glanced up and backed away at the same time. I knew that gesture well, too.

The boss had arrived. All these idiots were basically mirror images of Rocco's cronies, so naturally, I expected their chief to be more or less his clone.

No words in existence could define precisely how wrong I was.

11

"Who the hell am I looking at?" I jerked backward away from the window, and then leaned forward again very slowly until my forehead touched the glass. "That is definitely not a vampire."

On the contrary, the woman in the room was without a doubt the most beautiful I had ever seen. I had thought the guards were shrinking deliberately from her, but as she drew level with their position, I saw that she was just extremely tall. Long red hair, like the deep embers of a bonfire, framed her oval face in flowing rivulets. I swore she had a visible glow.

Not a vampire, no. But still not to be trusted. Marcus was not having any of this lady's undeniable badassery.

"No kidding." A little awestruck, I watched her move around the back of SplitScreen's chair. "I just want to know what her deal is. I've never seen anything like her before." He didn't answer me right away, and that gnawing curiosity refused to go away, so I prompted him again. "Hey, are you listening?"

Do not be seduced by this woman's beauty, Victoria. Not all monsters have fangs.

"Noted." I noticed the woman engaging SplitScreen in conversation. The words were ninety-nine percent inaudible, but I was still able to discern some of the expressions on their faces.

Boss lady started out friendly, handing out smiles that showed all her perfect teeth. But she wouldn't stop circling the chair like a shark around a sinking ship, and after Split-Screen failed to respond with the same warmth, the boss's demeanor slipped. She would occasionally turn her face toward the wall or toward one of the guards, and in those instances, I got a snapshot of a completely different person.

"Right," I said, frowning at the dark mask stretched across her otherwise flawless features. "I really hope she doesn't try to murder the blog chick. She looks like she can kick my ass." Not only did Marcus not dispute the statement, he didn't even make fun of me for making it.

That was when I started to worry.

The *Gladius Solis* still hung wrapped up in my bag, always ready for duty. "Marcus, if things turn ugly, do you think it's fine to just, like...whip the sword out in front of SplitScreen?" It was looking like we had no other choice, but everyone else who had seen the legendary weapon up to now had either known about it or ended up dead. "She's a blogger, Marcus. What if this gets out?"

Perhaps it is time. The entrance of the gods is imminent. The world must know there are instruments against them.

"What happened to not making our move until the gods

go public?" I kept my gaze fixed firmly on the scene inside the warehouse. The redhead was glowering now, her face a mask of frustration. We were running out of time.

Under present circumstances, I am afraid discretion cannot be helped. This child must be saved. And I believe that ensuring her salvation may grant us a certain amount of leverage over her sphere of influence, would it not?

Sometimes I forgot Marcus had a flair for strategy. Unable to deny most of his points, and increasingly convinced that things were going south on the other side of the window, I resolved to just cross the present bridge and handle the consequences later. That was my usual MO, after all.

"Dude, she's not a child," I scoffed. "You're only saying that because Gargantua in there would make Bigfoot look like a halfling." The next time I looked at SplitScreen, though, I found myself unable to deny that she *did* look little. Her voice hadn't sounded too young, but I could no longer be positive until I saw her face up close. "Dammit, she *better* not be a kid."

I told myself it didn't matter and forced the issue from my mind for the time being. Whatever her age, we had to get her out of there. If she was running some kind of scam on me, I could deal with that later. For now, I needed to keep SplitScreen alive.

On the other side of the gross window, the woman made one final orbit around the chair, her face marred by exceptional discontent. I still had no clue what SplitScreen had to say specifically, but it was not to her captor's liking. The fire-red mane of hair swished angrily as Gargantuan turned to her guards for a moment. Then, shooting the blogger one last, withering glare, she marched from the room.

Seventy feet away from me, the door to the warehouse swung open.

Acting on pure instinct, I dove for cover in the overgrown weeds, flattening myself as much as possible. I couldn't see her this way, but a velvety female voice drifted into my ear.

"The little one is no longer an issue mylady." Feet crunched on the gravel. A purring car pulled up, received its passengers, and pulled away. I leapt toward the window.

The guards remained in the empty room. One of them stood by the table now, casually loading a gun. He glanced over at SplitScreen, who sat with her head down, mouth still taped over.

It didn't take a rocket scientist to figure out what was coming next.

Hopping backward, I hefted a cinder block in both hands and hurled it through the glass. The other guard fired, but the sound of breaking glass surprised him, and his shot went wide, burying itself in the wall. SplitScreen flinched and hunched down lower in the chair. Strands of dark hair were falling from beneath her hat. I'd hoped she would look bigger, less utterly vulnerable, once I levered myself over the sill and into the same room as her. She did not. In fact, she appeared to be even tinier.

Another shot rang out. I heard the bullet zing past my head and into the floor. To my left, the first guard popped the last round into the chamber. He cocked back the hammer and leveled the barrel at me.

SplitScreen's shout was muffled through the tape, but it

sounded like, "No!" He was standing a little too close to her, and she lashed out with her boots just as he squeezed the trigger. He missed me, and like a bull, I put my head down and charged.

He attempted to get off one more shot, but I was faster. I slammed into him as he frantically hammered his finger on the trigger. In a second, the gun was in my hand. In two seconds, it was connecting rapidly with various parts of his face. In five, I spun around and chucked it viciously at the other guard, whose crooked nose exploded in a gush of blood.

He clapped his hands to his newly messed-up face, making a strained, honking wheeze through his fingers. It was almost too easy after that. He didn't even have the chance to guard his nuts before I kicked them back into his body. On the floor, the honking turned into more of a pathetic gurgle.

My work done, I turned to SplitScreen. The tape left a pink rectangle below her nose when I pulled it off.

"Son of a bitch, ow," she said. "But also, thank you."

"Don't thank me until this place is in the rearview mirror," I answered. "And maybe not even then." Using my pocket knife to cut her bindings, I pointed toward my original point of entry. "That way. I'll give you a boost."

She shook the blood back into her hands. "Are those guys gonna be okay?"

"You mean the assholes who kidnapped you?" I gave her a look. "Did you forget what just happened? They were totally going to shoot you."

She scowled. "Look, I'm always the girl behind the

curtain in case you haven't noticed. I just write about this shit… I didn't sign up for murder."

"Let me guess." I led her pointedly toward the window. "You have people who do that for you."

"Ha ha." She jumped up to grab the windowsill and let me push her the rest of the way. When we were both on the other side, she finished her thought. "No. I don't hurt people. I simply expose them."

"Right. And how was me telling you Silas Monk runs with vampires not exposing the *shit* out of him?"

SplitScreen pulled out her cellphone and punched a number into the keypad. "About that. I think I was wrong. If you have a minute, we should go somewhere and talk. For real this time."

"Okay, but it's gonna take more than a minute. And I have no idea where the hell we are, so we're going to need a car. How do you feel about hotwiring?"

"Don't worry about it." The blogger glanced at her phone. "I've got it covered." Two minutes later, a sleek silver sedan with tinted windows pulled into the lot. "Get in, and don't talk to the driver."

"Uh, fine?" I got in the back seat. An opaque partition separated the front and back. SplitScreen disappeared into the front passenger's side, leaving me alone in an odd cocoon of silence. We eased back out into traffic, and soon, the freeway streamed past the window.

I started to drowse a little, but then a thought torpedoed into my brain. I wrapped the medallion chain nervously around my finger. "Marcus?"

Victoria. I see your mission was successful.

"Do you think I screwed everything up by getting in her car?"

I doubt the recent victim of a kidnapping is going to turn around and kidnap you. He paused. *Besides, you are twice her size. You could easily overpower her.*

"That's true." I stared at the partition and pretended I knew where we were going. "I wonder what she's going to tell me." An image of red hair flashed through my mind's eye. It had been a long time since I'd met someone so intriguing. I already knew I didn't like her, but she was just inherently fascinating.

Like the next piece of a puzzle I was hell bent on solving.

THE CAR DROPPED us off outside of a sketchy little storefront with painted signs I couldn't read hanging in the windows. Realizing SplitScreen expected me to accompany her inside, I balked. She looked over her shoulder. "C'mon. I promise it's clean."

"Clean of what? And what is this place?"

"Bugs." She spoke with an air of forced patience, as if we had spontaneously swapped ages. "It's a net-café. I know the owners. And I don't want to stand around outside." With that, she went to the door and propped it open for me.

Do you want to make an ally out of this child or not? Marcus asked.

"You know what I want? I want you to call her a child

to her face. I have a feeling that's something I'd pay actual money to see."

Just go inside, Victoria.

I smirked, jogging a little to close the gap between us. "That means I win."

1 2

"I WANT TO MAKE SOMETHING CLEAR." SplitScreen sat across from me again, only this time, her face was in full view. Her huge brown eyes remained unnervingly steady on my face as she spoke, hardly even blinking. The hair I'd seen tumbling out of her hat turned out to be jet black and straight as a pin. "I'm just as paranoid as you, if not more. So, you can at least trust me as far as confidentiality is concerned. I have a blog, yeah, but I won't use it to sell you out." She chewed her lower lip. "I know how shitty that is."

"Fine." I decided I could live with that if it facilitated an open exchange of information. Trust never came easy, but I was in a damned tight spot. "Do you care if I ask you some questions, then? I don't mind working with you as long as it benefits both of us, but I'm not super into the whole cloak and dagger bit. Riding in that car was like solitary confinement."

She turned a little sheepish. "Sorry. Maybe it's sort of over the top, but when I started writing the articles about

Monk, you know what happened? My inbox filled up with threats, people asking where I lived, people saying they'd find and kill me. So, these days, I feel it's necessary to take some extra precautions."

"Hold up. Death threats? I feel like I'm missing something. Why is this rich nerd such a threat?"

"Have you never seen a Bond movie? Rich nerds are always trying to blow up the moon or some shit." She opened an ornate little bottle, which she poured into a square cup. The liquid was strong enough that I smelled it from my seat, like flowers soaked in mean booze.

"And he's more than just that anyway. More than what people think. And that's the problem." She lifted the cup to her lips and sipped it delicately. "He's walking down a dangerous path. And rubbing shoulders with some real asshats along the way."

The scent of her drink both burned and delighted my nose. It sucked all the excitement out of my regular stout. "What sort of dangerous path, and why do you care? The dude's a freaking billionaire. Something tells me you don't run in the same circles."

"Are you kidding?" She huffed. "He revolutionized my industry. Monk has everything to do with me. He is the reason we're sitting here today, right here, right now." A beat passed. She let out her breath. "Do you want some *sake*? You might need it if you want me to tell you everything."

"That's what this stuff is?"

"Yeah. I'll only pour you a little to start. It's an acquired taste." She poured what looked like three drops into a cup and pushed it across to me. "So, a few years back, I was a recently graduated computer science major from Stanford. My dream was to be at the absolute forefront of the technological world. It wasn't enough to be on the cutting edge. I wanted to be the one creating it." A wry smile curved her mouth. "What better way to realize that dream than to pack it to Palo Alto after I got my degree, right? There were things being developed here that couldn't even have been imagined anywhere else. A utopian enclave of geniuses."

The smile turned bitter. "I was naïve. I really thought this place was full of visionaries, innovators, and people who wanted to make the best version of the future come true. But then I got here and took a job at this startup that was pitching a way to redefine communications. The way people thought. The way people saw themselves, saw each other. What an amazing new Earth that would be."

"I'm guessing it was all bunk." The tiny sip of *sake* I'd just taken burned down my throat like sweet fire. I swore I felt it land in my stomach.

"Not all of it." She stared into her square cup. "But there was a lot—most of it—that they didn't tell us, such as what they meant by 'communications.' The company grew like crazy, and a couple years in, I found out our main source of income was mining and selling customers' data. I mean millions of people who just became commodities. Everything they were, and everything they wished they weren't, out there for someone to buy. Just so they could market stupid shit even better."

"Pretty slimy," I remarked. It was the best response I could muster, my own sense of ethics having been dulled by my thirst for vengeance. "So, you quit?"

"Of course, I quit!" She glared at nothing in particular. "They don't give a shit about people in Silicon Valley. All they care about is money and ownership."

"Sounds about right." I drank the last two drops of *sake* and switched back to my beer, which tasted like water in comparison. "It's like that in New York, too."

"It's like that everywhere. Which is why I started my blog, to expose that kind of garbage." Suddenly, she blinked. "Wait, you came here from New York? That's a long way just to talk." Her hands steepled beneath her chin. "I spilled my story. Why the hell are *you* here?"

I leaned back in my chair. "I'll just throw you in the deep end and see if you can swim. My parents are dead, and while I was chasing the guy who killed them, I got wrapped up in some truly unbelievable shit. The kind of thing you dream about after eating pizza at midnight."

I expected her to jump on that, but she let a moment of stillness filter through the air. "I'm sorry about your parents."

"Don't apologize," I said. It wasn't necessarily the correct response, but defusing the awkwardness that came with any explanation of my current state of affairs was second nature to me.

"I want to," she said. "My parents are really, well, important to me."

We were quiet then, not looking at each other. "Thanks," I told her finally. "It was five years ago. I'm working through it. And honestly, it sort of helps that my life's gone off the rails since then."

"Then, I'm… glad?" She smirked. "Is this where the vampires come in?"

I raised my eyebrows and grinned. "Yeah...turns out they're real. And worse. It's basically my new life's calling to stop them."

"So you're like Buffy the Vampire Slayer?"

I rolled my eyes—I knew that joke would get old fast.

"Yeah, something like that. And I have reason to believe they're somehow tied to Monk Industries."

"Why? Because of that story I wrote about the exsanguinations?" She poured more sake for both of us. "I'm not saying I believe you, but it's no less insane than some of the stuff I know is actually happening in the Valley. It's like, if Monk can build a weapon that will potentially solve the energy crisis forever, why can't there be a bunch of blood-crazed weirdos with fangs running around? The threshold for normality gets lower every day."

"Run that by me again? Silas Monk is doing *what*?" All of my senses perked up.

"No one knows for sure yet, but I've been around a while, and I've done my research on him. He's always talking about trying to change the way we use energy on Earth." The blogger's dark eyes lit up with a keen spark of excitement. "And he's spoken a lot in recent months about geothermal methods specifically. It's complicated, of course, but the simple explanation is that energy drawn from deep within the planet is a renewable resource and could theoretically replace all of our current finite sources like fossil fuels. Which is basically saying it has the potential to save the planet, and therefore, save humanity."

"I'm sensing a catch," I said, signaling for another beer. This was one of those times where I didn't want to be hammered inside of half an hour, and I didn't trust the *sake* not to do that. "And I noticed that you called this thing a weapon, not a tool."

"Yeah. Monk has always been shady, but recently he's changed. His clothes, the way he talks, the people he interacts with. Monk's been screwing around with weapons' contractors on the side. He thinks he's being discreet, but I mean, the evidence is all over if you know where to look. We've even uncovered a possible code name. Light." She shrugged. "Most likely an acronym for something."

The entire planet screeched to a halt. Everything dissolved except me, this stranger whose life I'd just saved, and the mental videotape of that vamp in the alley, talking at me through two major holes in his mouth. *Pretty soon, we're gonna have a light of our own.* His words ambled through my head, over and over.

My brain told me the connection was a stretch at best, but a tiny little voice in the back of my head, the one I associated with my instincts, refused to let it go. A light of their own. No, not light, but LIGHT. All caps.

How could it be a coincidence?

"Interesting," I said, so as not to be silent for too long. "Any guesses what it might be?"

Are you thinking what I am thinking, Victoria? Marcus inquired.

I nodded slightly, pretending it was to myself as I considered everything SplitScreen had said. On the inside, my head spun like a carnival ride. This was it—this *had* to be it. The reason mobsters were being shipped out West, never to return. The reason things were so damned quiet in New York as of late. All the baddies were flocking here to get a load of the brand-new toy they were about to nab from the humans.

"I don't want to contribute too much to base conjecture," the blogger said. "It can be risky to put too much of this stuff out there. Besides, Monk is set to present something at the Global Tech Expo next week—something big, by the sounds of it."

"The weapon."

"It might not be a weapon," she said.

"You don't buy that."

She leaned forward. "Listen. The death threats I was getting? They started when I was writing about Codename: LIGHT, whatever it is. I'm paranoid, but I'm not an idiot. There's something going on here, and I need to know what it is."

Spoken like a smart girl after my own heart. I sat up straight and looked her dead in the eye. "One last thing."

"Shoot."

"I need to ask you about what went down in that warehouse. I'm sorry if it's too soon, but that woman and her lackeys obviously meant business, and I have to know what that business was. What did she say to you?"

The blogger fell silent for a few seconds, studying a point on the wall over my shoulder. When she spoke again, her voice was very quiet. "I'm not afraid of much," she said. "But she freaked me the hell out." Her eyes suddenly snapped to my face, full of burning intensity. "If you know her, tell me who she is. Just because I didn't crack the first time doesn't mean she won't come back for me."

"I have no clue who she is. I was hoping she gave you a hint."

SplitScreen frowned. "All she wanted to talk about was that damn drill. What I knew. What I'd heard. What I was planning to 'release,' as she put it. She wanted to know if I was a threat."

"Are you?" I asked.

SplitScreen smiled. "If I wasn't before, I am now."

Staring into her stony, defiant expression, I saw no hints of deception, and even though I'd already seen her champion level poker face in action, it was a lot easier to believe her when I could actually see her face. "Alright. Looks like we're on the same side of this one. But if we're going to work together, I need to know your name. Split-Screen was fine until you got a face."

"Oh!" Her pale cheeks pinked a little. "Namiko."

"A mononym?" I grinned. "Does that make you an artist?"

She snorted. "You didn't tell me you were gonna make fun of it."

"It's cool," I said. "I got one, too. It's Vic."

I put my hand out. Namiko took it carefully. We shook.

"Here's to the beginning of a beautiful friendship," she said.

13

Namiko's phone vibrated as she was using it to call her car. She read the notification without saying a word, but then her hand reached out and gripped my arm. "You're not going to believe this."

"What?" I steeled myself for news of the earth splitting open or another golden meteorite crash landing in San Francisco Bay.

"The news just broke. Monk decided to move up his reveal. Guess he's just too excited to wait until next week." This last sentence fairly dripped disdain.

"*What?*" I asked. "When?"

Namiko pursed her lips. "Tonight. Tech Institute of San Francisco. Invitation only."

"Well, I know what I'm doing tonight." I ran a hand through my hair and frowned. "I should probably take a shower first, huh?"

My new friend laughed. "Yeah, right, Vic. Do you know

how totally exclusive these things are? I have a whole web of connections, and I wouldn't be able to get in."

"Good thing I'm not you, then," I said cheerfully. The silver sedan slipped into the lot.

"Hilarious. Really though, you don't get it. They won't even look at you if you're not on the list." She held the door open and then got into the back beside me. "Better come up with a plan B."

"And miss this golden opportunity to see everything up close and personal? No way in hell. There must be some way to hack the system, right?"

"Maybe you should ask a hacker," she retorted. "Although...hang on." She entrenched herself in her phone for a minute. Then she held it up so I could see the screen. "Do you think you could pretend to be her?"

"What?" In hindsight, I probably should have seen this coming, but in the moment, I was totally blindsided. "Who's that?"

I pointed at the picture of the woman with long, dark hair and green eyes. We shared the same complexion, but the similarities didn't go *much* further.

"Her name is Monica Tellenburg. She's a tech journo, which means we have the same job, except hers is above board. She's one of the top writers for the biggest tech site out there. And *that* means she is going to be at the event tonight."

"How do you know that?" The picture of Namiko's plan was beginning to form in my mind. I had never engaged in that sort of actual espionage before, but if it would get me closer to Monk and his secret weapon, I was already warming to the idea.

"Oh, please. They wouldn't miss this scoop if their lives depended on it."

"And how exactly am I going to get in under her name? If she's a big shot, they'll recognize her, won't they?"

"'Big-shot' is a relative term in our field. She might technically be more successful than me, but she's not even orbiting these guys' pay grade. Most of them know her name, maybe they've seen her headshot." She looked at the picture and then up at me. "I mean, you're a couple of all-American white girls. How hard could it be? As long as you get there first, you can slip in. I can call someone who'll make it a little easier. Deal?"

I pressed my lips together. "This is our best bet, huh?"

"Unless you have a better idea, yeah. Also, I'll give Monica an offer she can't refuse."

Raising an eyebrow, I responded. "You deal in threats in the blogosphere?"

Namiko laughed. "Hardly. I have a scoop on a new driverless car tech that I got the first leak on. I'll offer her that, in exchange for her not showing up at the expo tonight. It's a pretty huge scoop. She'd be crazy not to take it." She pressed down a silver button in the backseat with her thumb. "Drop my friend off at The Crown, please."

For the first time, I examined the interior of the car—all white leather seats and wood accents. "Real wood?"

She tapped the button. "And real silver. What's the point in being *bougie* if you're not going to take it all the way?"

I laughed. "Don't take *this* the wrong way, but how can you afford it if you're living on the fringes of society as an outcast blogger?"

Namiko sighed. "It's a weird dichotomy. My dad does import/export over in Japan. Suffice it to say, he makes bank. I don't really like to flaunt it on the outside. Most of the things that I have, I earned myself. That distinction is critical to me. I need to feel like I'm playing an active role in my own life." She thought for a minute. "It's also important to note: I attended Stanford on a full-ride scholarship. My father did not pay my way. But now...let's just say that he believes in the good that I do."

So, she made up for her miniscule stature with a brain five times the size of mine. I tried not to think about the last time I did real math. "That's cool. I'm glad you're on my side."

"You know what?" she said. "I think I'm glad, too." The silver sedan cruised to a slow stop outside the front of my motel. I moved to get out, and Namiko stopped me. "Oh, I almost forgot. Silas Monk has a new lady in his life. You might want to keep an eye on her."

I do not recall any mention of a partner in your research, Marcus piped up. Of course, he'd want to talk about the girlfriend.

Still, his sentiments were worth paraphrasing. "I didn't know Monk had a girlfriend."

"That's the thing. He didn't up until a few weeks ago. Now, he's got this hot model glued to his side. He hasn't made a single public appearance alone since he met her."

"Maybe they're in love," I quipped.

"Uh huh. Or maybe one of them is hiding something." Her face eased into a small smile. "Good luck, Vic. I'll contact you later with details on your admission. I'm rooting for you."

Among the surreal landscape that continued to be my life, it felt strange to have sort of made a friend. I took a quick shower, resisting the urge to soak in the actual bathtub, and pulled on the clothes I grabbed from the store beside the hotel. White blouse. Charcoal pants. Black pumps. They would have to do.

As an afterthought, I used the motel's wall-mounted dryer on my hair, carefully brushing out every errant snarl. If Namiko was right about the status of this event, then I needed to be sure I was as divorced as possible from my true identity.

"What do you think?" I asked Marcus as I stood in front of the full-length mirror on the bathroom door. "Nice enough? Or do I look like a poser?"

You're not Cleopatra, but we have no choice but to hope this disguise is sufficient, he replied. *Your usual boorish ways are off limits tonight.*

I grabbed my bag off the back of the hotel chair. "Did you hear that? That's the sound of me never asking for your opinion again." Satisfied that I had everything I needed to fake my way through the night, I sat down on the edge of the bed with my phone in my hand to wait for Namiko's message.

Are you prepared for this, Victoria? Marcus asked. *It is something of an unusual undertaking.*

"It'll be...fine." I hoped that projecting an aura of confidence would make my words true. "I wanna know what you think about that woman. The tall one with the red hair. Other than the fact that I shouldn't trust her; I got that part."

It is hard to pinpoint her nature, except to say she is clearly a creature of deceit...and likely also one of significant power. Not every Forgotten appears as the monster they are, you know. And not every battle requires a sword.

"I—" My phone went off with a message from Namiko: **Monica took my deal. Get there early. You're going to get 'recognized.' Pick up her press pass. Boom.**

It all seemed straightforward enough. I stood up, checked my reflection one last time. "Let's get this shit show on the road."

THE SAN FRANCISCO TECH INSTITUTE was a marvel of modern engineering set like a diamond in the middle of its meticulously groomed campus, all sparkling glass and sleek metal. A red carpet had been rolled out from the main entrance of the built-in conference hall, all the way down to the curb. I had asked the cab driver to let me out two blocks away, and the walk over gave me a full view of the technological elite stepping out in their finest evening wear.

I glanced down at my outfit. "Definitely a poser."

Your words, not mine.

It didn't really matter. There was no way I could pass as an actual invited guest anyway. The success of this night hinged heavily on Namiko's help, and to a somewhat lesser extent, my capacity for stealth and cunning, neither of which I had honed much in recent days, beyond the occasional takedown of inattentive guards and a few surly vampires.

So, I was already off to a promising start.

I picked up my pace as I wove into the edge of the throng gathered alongside the red carpet. Namiko had said I'd get recognized, but neglected to provide further details. What exactly did she mean? I kept my eyes peeled for a plant—if there was one, they'd have to be somewhere out here, on the border of the event itself. Photographers jockeyed for space along the velvet rope perimeter, calling out to the rich and famous in hopes of snapping the perfect shot.

Still constantly on the move, I leaned in to see if I could catch a glimpse of Silas Monk. His bland, face barely stood out in my memory. Would he look different in front of the lens? Would there be some miraculous transformation to reflect his wealth and intellect in the eyes of the public?

Probably not. I fully expected him to step onto the makeshift catwalk looking like the universe's most illustrious geometry teacher, because in this part of the country, the nerds were the rock stars.

A matte black limousine purred up to the sidewalk, causing the crowd to hush for a second. I got bumped in the shoulder by an eager dude in a bowtie and a jacket that didn't fit his skinny arms.

"Sorry," he said, looking at me a little too long. "Hey, do I—"

"Monica? Monica, over here!" Since my name isn't Monica, it took me a few to realize that the call was directed at me. "Monica! Come pick up your press pass! You're gonna be late!"

I shot a look at the guy calling me, intending to confirm that he had identified the wrong person with the right intentions, but he just beckoned insistently and then disappeared into the crowd. Not much of a failsafe, but I guessed I'd never really had one. Namiko had been very clear on the whole 'no promises' thing.

"You're press, right?" asked the guy with the skinny arms. "Lucky." He did his best to approximate a suave smirk. "Do you think you could sneak me in? I'll make it worth your while."

I commanded my facial muscles not to organize themselves in any configuration resembling disgust. "Sorry, pal. I didn't get a plus-one." Before he had the chance to reply, I waded off in the direction where the guy had motioned for me to go. There was a table outside the conference center's ticket office manned by a fearsomely put-together middle-aged woman.

"Media?" she asked. There were only a few media cards left unclaimed, which she had fanned in front of her on the tabletop. I scanned them quickly with my eyes. Thankfully, there was only one Monica.

"Monica Tellenburg."

She sifted through the IDs, barely double-checking with a quick glance at my face. I put on as much nonchalance as I could muster. "Here you are, dear. Better get in there quick. I think it's going to be quite full tonight."

Somewhat startled by the simplicity of the ruse, I thanked her and walked away. In line to enter the special side door, I checked the credentials she'd given me, and I had to do a double take myself. As it turned out, Monica Tellenburg *did* look like me. No wonder Namiko had singled her out so quickly. A twinge of guilt poked at my stomach.

"Thanks, Monica," I whispered. "I hope you nail the driverless car story."

I am sure she will make the most of the information on the steel monsters that lack a charioteer.

"Do me a favor and keep it quiet tonight?" I said. "I'm gonna need to concentrate, and it's hard to do that with some smartass talking in my head."

Noted. I will only speak to notify you of your mistakes.

"Oh, that's perfect."

<hr>

THE INSIDE of the conference center looked like it was made of jewels. Points of light reflected off the glass and stone façade like stars on the polished floor. Soft piano music piped through hidden speakers as impeccably dressed waiters circulated with the fanciest appetizer trays I'd ever seen. I kept my head on a permanent swivel, scouring the glammed-out room for signs of Monk, who'd escaped my scrutiny by slipping in during my press badge adventure.

It didn't take me long to locate the press table during my circuit of the room, but I did my best to stay away from that area. Our little trick had fooled that woman at check-in, but I had a feeling it wouldn't work as well around the actual press, particularly if there was anyone over there who knew Monica Tellenburg in real life. Hell, I wasn't even sure I'd be able to bluff my way through small talk. I'd never been much for extended improv.

The party itself wasn't altogether unpleasant. Among the legitimate guests, I felt woefully underdressed, but everyone was either too polite or too intent on getting sloshed on the free high-end booze to notice me slowly circling the room. My first sighting of Monk happened on the third or fourth pass and only because my ears caught a woman's voice gushing, "Oh, Mr. Monk, you're *just* as delightful as I imagined!"

Surreptitiously, I turned to see the back of a trim figure in a dark blue suit, his arm around the waist of an hourglass in red. He was nothing like the nerd-turned businessman that I expected from his photos. And as Namiko had said, his new girlfriend appeared to be physically affixed to his side. A sweep of gold bangles on both wrists matched the rich twist in her hair. Her perfect manicure stood out brightly against the dark shade of Monk's suit. They were both laughing.

She started to turn her head in my direction.

My whole body pivoted as I looked away toward the empty stage. We had just barely missed making eye contact, but I could feel her gaze linger on me for a second or two, as if she'd known it was me watching her. Part of me wanted to turn back toward her as a challenge, but the risk was too great. I was there for recon only, not to make a scene.

Despite that, just the shadow of her glance chilled me to the bone. I shivered. Why the hell was she looking at me? Why did I feel like she could see through me? There was absolutely something going on with Monk's new squeeze, and I wasn't sure I really wanted to know what it was.

Plainly speaking, she freaked me out. The next time I

spotted a waiter holding water glasses, I flagged him down, took one, and downed half of it in one gulp.

How are you feeling? Good old Marcus, just checking in. *You look shaken.*

"I think I might be in over my head," I whispered, so softly there was almost no sound.

You know what they say, he answered. *Sink or swim.*

14

By the time Monk actually got up to do his thing, I had acclimated somewhat to the atmosphere of the gala. To my immense relief, the real press had dispersed rapidly throughout the crowd, seeking quotes and sound bites from the biggest stars. They paid no attention to me.

When my feet got tired of methodically circling, I found a seat in an inconspicuous corner and took it, content to wait for the main event. Eventually, the lights in the hall flickered a few times and dimmed, and a guy in a silvery white ensemble got up to make introductions.

He spoke for about four minutes, during which, by my estimation, he said absolutely nothing. It was easy to see the version of Silicon Valley that Namiko saw now that I was surrounded by it. Dozens and dozens of ludicrously wealthy mavens only concerned with belongings.

"This is a man who has built an empire out of nothing but a few simple pages of code, a man who formed diamonds from sand. He stands before you all tonight as the greatest, proudest innovator of his time. Ladies and gentlemen, I give you Silas Monk!"

The crowd, which had been mercifully subdued up to this point, erupted into a dignified roar. Monk took the stage like a real celebrity, smiling and waving, posing for a few well-timed cameras. Unsurprisingly, he was not alone. The woman in the red dress hung delicately on his arm. She smiled, too, but she didn't make any attempt to draw undue attention to herself.

She didn't need to. My false brothers and sisters in the media devoured her. The image of Silas Monk, tech star extraordinaire, paired off with a perfect blonde bombshell was too good to resist. I supposed if I was in their shoes, I'd be excited about it, too, but as an observer, the whole spectacle just sort of rubbed me the wrong way. It felt too much like a put-on.

To Monk's credit, some of that feeling went away when he began to speak—but only some. The fact that his girlfriend sat perched in a chair just to the side of the podium detracted from the impact of his words. Half the men and a fair number of the women in his audience only had eyes for her.

Monk himself was possessed of a certain kind of awkward charm. His enthusiasm was so potent that it was difficult not to get caught up in it. He paced excitedly around the stage, talking with his hands, even jumping up and down a little bit.

"I can't tell you how privileged and grateful I feel to be able to share these incredible advancements with you tonight. We are on the cusp of something truly life-changing, not just for the lucky few here in this room, but for every man, woman, and child on Earth. While it is indisputable that we live in a time of frequent uncertainty, I am beyond proud to announce to you tonight that those uncertainties will soon come to an end.

"My developer and I have poured our blood, sweat, and tears into the creation of the future; indeed, into the salvation of mankind. It is my esteemed pleasure to present this gift, so long in the making, tonight."

The lights went down, and a tense murmur ran through the onlookers. As the lights came up again, a sheer curtain dropped from the back of the stage, and something mounted atop a heavy square pedestal came rolling forward, draped in a shroud. Silas Monk took the woman in red by the hand, and together, they each grasped a corner of the covering. Cameras flashed. He threw the captive crowd a wide, sweaty grin.

"For too long, humanity has toiled in the darkness. Now," he announced. "Behold the LIGHT!"

The shroud fluttered down to the stage, revealing an object in a thick glass case. It was smaller than I'd anticipated, and from my vantage point, I couldn't really tell what it was supposed to be. The guests at the front sent up a dutiful cheer, and there was quite a bit of chatter from the experts in the room.

Monk stood beside his latest gadget beaming, his arm once more locked around the blonde's waist. Her facial expression hadn't budged an inch, but her eyes picked over the crowd.

I made sure not to look at her for more than a few seconds at a time. The prospect of making eye contact filled me with dread, which was doubly upsetting because I didn't know why. Keeping my head down, I joined the waves of curious spectators moving up to get a closer look at the LIGHT.

I never got nearer than three rows back from the stage, but by then, I could ascertain that it was, in fact, some sort of drill, albeit one I'd never seen before. The slot for the bit seemed impossibly thin, and I thought I could see something glowing down in the mechanism of the device.

A slew of diagrams were brought out on boards and easels, ostensibly in order to explain how the thing worked, but they were one hundred percent inscrutable to me. Combined with the constant camera flashes, I was starting to get one killer headache.

Monk waved his hands at the advancing throng, grinning with delight at the palpable excitement in the room. "Ladies and gentlemen, I must implore you to wait a moment," he said, putting on airs. "You see, we're not quite done here." The crowd murmured. Monk stepped back toward the glass case. "In fact, I would consider what you're about to see the main event of our little soiree. I couldn't leave tonight without a demonstration, could I?"

You could've heard a pin drop in the atrium. The hinges on the back of the case squeaked in the dead silence as Monk reached in and released the securing anchors. The glass lifted away, leaving the device naked on its pedestal. At the same time, a huge, thick sheet of apparent stone or metal came down on a heavy-duty apparatus to be positioned in front of the drill.

Monk put on a pair of tinted goggles. A sheer curtain dropped down in front of the drill's bit path. "And then," he intoned, "there was LIGHT." He flipped a switch on the side of the instrument. A glow began in its bowels. I heard the distinct sound of a mechanism spooling up.

It was hard to describe what happened next. The curtain seemed to flash and ripple, and a plume of sudden smoke erupted around the target slab. When it cleared, a clean hole stood out in the center.

Monk turned to the audience and bowed. A beat later, the applause began. My brain, still wrapping itself around the brief spectacle I'd just witnessed, throbbed with the effort.

"I need some air," I whispered to Marcus. "Let's go."

THE CONFERENCE CENTER had a row of side doors that opened on a garden promenade. I stepped out onto the walk, deeply inhaling the crisp night air. The stars were out in full force, as much as they were ever out in the heart of the city, but the breeze had a bite that was enough to keep most of the attendees inside. Personally, I found both the temperature and the solitude extremely refreshing.

"So, what do you think?" I asked my medallion, making sure to face out toward the lush garden so that no one could see me talking to myself. "Weapon of the gods or just Palo Alto's latest modern gem?"

Not a weapon yet, but it could be formidable if it got into the wrong hands.

"I think one of those diagrams said there's a laser in it." I fished my phone out of my bag. "Gonna have to go back in and snap a few photos. Namiko'll be all over this."

I am glad you have found a living ally, however temporary. Your quest is brave, but lonely.

"It's… it's not that lonely. Plus, I get to do cool shit like crash this party pretty much all the time now. And Lord knows *you're* never going anywhere."

Deep down, though, I kind of agreed. Having someone to share the experience helped me feel like I was finally getting to move past the darkest phase of my life. Vic Stratton, Emo Vigilante, was emerging from her cocoon to become Vic Stratton, Hunter of Gods.

That had a pretty nice ring to it.

* * *

I WASN'T sure how long I stayed out there, but I had a miniature heart attack when someone called to me. "Miss?"

My whole body froze, a million different scenarios spinning through my head. A million ways I could have messed up. My first thought was that Monica Tellenburg had turned up and wanted revenge. But the guy trying to get my attention was just a friendly staff member.

"I wanted to make sure you were all right," he said. "And let you know the reception is starting if you'd like to come in and get a drink."

Would I ever.

"You're too kind," I said, stepping away from the railing. "I guess I did lose track of time. I just came out for some air." None of that was technically untrue. Being present at this event was, I suspected, likely very similar to being a human inside Carcerum: beautiful people, lavish displays of wealth, and a pervasive sense that you do not belong.

"I understand, miss." He chuckled. "It's awfully full in here tonight. Hope you enjoy the rest of your evening."

He left as abruptly as he had arrived, and I let the crowd carry me back toward the stage. The LIGHT drill itself was gone, obviously, but the diagrams remained. Snapping a photo of each, I put away my phone and headed toward the bar.

Now that I'd seen the great invention, it was time to get close to the mastermind.

For a larger than life, celebrity tech guru, Silas Monk sure knew how to blend in. I first tried to locate him by tracking down areas with the loudest noise, but that seemed to just show me who was the drunkest. Then I tried looking for dark blue suits, but there were a thousand of those. Ultimately, it was the red dress that I spotted, practically exploding in a sea of sensible shades. And of course, Monk had his arm wrapped around her.

Hmm. Marcus chose not to elaborate, so I didn't press him. Instead, I started gently pushing my way toward Monk's location, tracking him through glimpses of that scarlet fabric. I knew I was getting close when I could hear the blonde's gold bangles jingling along the length of her arm

All of a sudden, I had broken through some sort of invisible people barrier, and I stood face to face with her, not a single person between us. There was an extreme familiarity about her that I couldn't pinpoint until I realized she was tall. Too tall, really.

She smiled at me with her perfect teeth. "I don't think we've been introduced, have we?"

"No." My voice came out as an anxious caricature of itself. "Not yet."

"My name is Eve." She appraised me thoroughly. "I love your sweater. Come, sit down and have a drink.

"Oh, I'm all right." I shifted my weight from one foot to the other. "I was just wondering if I might have a chance to speak with Mr. Monk? I'm a huge fan of his work."

The woman laughed softly. "Of course you are, darling. *Everyone* is." She glanced over one slender shoulder. "I'm afraid Silas is terribly busy at the moment, but I'm sure he won't be too much longer. You're welcome to wait here with me if you like. Then you'll be sure to catch his attention."

"Right." The whole interaction made me feel like I wanted to jump out of my skin. My gaze moved restlessly around the room, lighting on everything except her face. But I couldn't stay away from it forever. Eventually, our eyes happened to lock for the tiniest fraction of a second.

I instantly forgot why I hadn't liked her before. She was so sweet, so welcoming, so safe. Who was I to deny her generous offer of a drink at the bar? The whole purpose of this little adventure was to gather information, right? And what better way to do it than networking with Silas Monk's constant companion?

If there was a Nobel Prize for investigation, I deserved it.

"Tell me about yourself," Eve encouraged. "You're so *young* to have been invited to one of Silas's galas. It's very impressive."

Her voice bubbled like newly poured champagne, and I suddenly felt very warm—like someone was wrapping me in a thick blanket. A buzzing sound seemed to fill the room, drowning out any voice but hers.

Without thinking, I answered, "Oh, I wouldn't say I was invited."

Victoria, Marcus cautioned.

I scrambled for damage control. "I have a press ID. I'm just… not on the official guest list."

"Is this your passion then? Tech journalism? If so, it must have been very exciting to watch Silas unveil the machine that's going to change the world."

I smiled widely. "This has been the best night of my life. The only thing that could make it better is a real interview with the most famous genius on Earth."

Eve laughed. It was a sound like falling water. "You are just darling. What's your name?" She accepted a drink from the bartender and offered it to me. "Please, I insist."

I hesitated, but it didn't last long. One drink would barely register. "Thank you. I'm Vic."

"Vic? That must be short for something. Victoria, perhaps?"

The name I had so deliberately abandoned sounded brand new—at least coming from someone other than Marcus. "Yeah, that's right."

"May I call you Victoria instead? It's such a beautiful name. One I would consider for my own daughter."

Victoria? Marcus's voice rattled in my head.

I sent Marcus a barrage of psychic messages to can it and let me handle things. I was doing great on my own, paving a way to my real target. The more Eve warmed up to me, the easier it would be to access Monk, preferably one on one. All I had to do was keep her focused on me until he appeared.

Then, almost out of nowhere, there he was. That dark blue suit obviously cost more money than I had ever earned in my entire life, and it was tailored expertly to fit his form. His unremarkable face notwithstanding, he was like a living catalog picture, at once a pioneer and the industry's clean-cut golden boy.

It was a powerful image.

Monk sat himself down on Eve's opposite side, directing a smile and a vaguely friendly nod my way. I wanted to get up and maneuver myself beside him so that I might have the chance to ask a few questions, but the weight of a finely manicured hand fell on my knee. Each tapered nail was deep blood red.

Victoria, I think it is time to leave.

I glanced up into Eve's beautiful, still-smiling face and decided Marcus was wrong. Just because I hadn't been able to talk to Silas Monk didn't mean I had to bail already. This was a slow burn kind of deal. It required patience and finesse, two things Marcus didn't always have.

So, I ignored him. An hour passed, and then another. Marcus periodically tried to get my attention, but I pushed him away and kept talking to Eve. I told her I was from New York. She told me she hadn't spent a lot of time there —which struck me as odd for such a glamorous woman— and that she'd love to hear more about it.

Every so often, she interrupted my stories to check and see if Monk was available to join in the conversation, but he had always just been snagged by someone else, or he was talking to a reporter, or in the midst of procuring another round for a group of guests.

And before I knew it, the conference center was closing down, and I was in a cab going back to the motel. That was when it hit me that I never spoke to Monk at all.

Not a single word.

15

My sleep after the gala was strangely heavy and deep, like I had gone to bed beneath a weighted blanket. The drapes, wine-colored and thick enough to shield me from the prying eyes of truck headlights, blocked out nearly every iota of sunlight that passed through the window on the other side. When I finally forced my eyes open at ten in the morning, the room was as dark as a subterranean cave.

I sort of liked it. Amid the hectic insanity that characterized my version of business as usual, lying around in the dark like a human-shaped rock was a nice change of pace. I indulged myself in twenty minutes of undiluted peace. Then I reached across to the nightstand with the alarm clock on it, grasped Marcus's medallion, and dragged it over my head.

"G'morning," I mumbled.

Fine morning, Victoria. How was your rest?

I rubbed a hand over my face. "I dunno, dude. I feel kind of loopy today."

I do not recall you imbibing too many beverages.

"Hell, no. I only had the one from…" I frowned. "What was her name? The woman in the dress. Monk's girl-friend." Troubling blank spots surfaced in my memory when I examined the reception after Monk's speech. She had told me her name; I knew she did. But it was just out of my reach.

Eve, said Marcus helpfully.

A connection completed in my brain, clearing away a little bit of the fog. "Yes! Eve. She gave me the only drink I had last night." I studied the shadows lurking on the motel ceiling. "You don't think she drugged me, do you?" Why was it so hard to remember?

Doubtful. I was vigilant all night. But I would suggest that you exercise caution around her in the future. You were…very open about who you are. That doesn't seem like a wise approach.

"I mean, she definitely had her boobs done." Hauling myself reluctantly into an upright position, I ran my tongue over my teeth. The inside of my mouth tasted like a dry sock. "What the *hell*? I'm officially too old for parties."

The blurriness surrounding my conversations with Eve still needled me as I trudged into the bathroom to wash my face and brush my teeth. I sat at that bar for hours and still managed to miss the star of the evening entirely—because I was talking to his girlfriend?

None of that really made sense to me, but I wasn't awake enough to piece anything together. I just went and sat on the edge of the bed. Then, a definite recollection sprang into my mind. I extracted my phone from my purse on the chair and checked the camera roll. Sure enough, the pictures I'd taken of Monk's onstage diagrams were there. I put them in an email to Namiko with the subject line: **Look what I got!**

She replied in less than a minute: **Meet at your motel in 15??**

I grinned. She was either ravenously interested, jealous, or both.

Part of me hoped for a little bit of both.

Namiko knocked on my door in fifteen minutes flat, and when I answered, she was back to being a pair of outlandishly huge, reflective sunglasses wedged in a pile of assorted fabric. She looked both ways along the bank of rooms prior to stepping into mine. Only then did she pull down the scarf. "You can never be too careful."

I nodded and made sure the door locked behind her. We sat in the dark with the bedside lamp on while she poured over my photos.

"I don't suppose he demonstrated it, did he?" she asked.

"Yeah, he sure did. He demonstrated the hell out of it." I pulled up the diagrams on my own phone. "Turns out the laser at its core has some kick."

"Wow. That's...bold. He just fired it off? Nothing between you and it?" I shook my head, she shook hers. "That must be their solution to the problem of melting drill bits." She pursed her lips. "But that could also make this thing exceptionally dangerous if the beam is amplified and used for destructive purposes." She turned to me then, her huge eyes deadly serious. "Vic, I have something to tell you."

A tiny chill ran through my bones, but I made my outward mannerisms remain calm. "What's up?"

"Someone came to visit me after I returned from our meeting yesterday. His timing was rather suspect."

I felt my teeth set themselves on edge. "Who? A man?"

"Yes. A bit strange-looking, but hey, San Francisco is a weird place, right? Originally, I wasn't going to let him through the gate, but he asked me a question that I thought you should know about." She paused thoughtfully, the tips of two fingers pressed in the hollow of her chin. "He wanted to know Silas Monk's address."

"Oh," I said. "That's not good. What did this guy look like?"

Namiko scowled. "He gave me the creeps. He was like three times my size, and he was wearing dark glasses, gloves, and a trench coat. Didn't stay long enough for me to get a read on him. I think he was carrying something, but I can't be sure."

"Something like a weapon?" I asked.

"Maybe, yeah. In one of those holsters across his back. I thought I saw a handle when he turned around."

"Huh. Did you tell him where Monk is?"

"Of course not. Said I didn't know, which is true. He doesn't publicize his personal information. And now we know why."

"We also have to get to him before this guy does. I guess he could just be a weirdo superfan, but let's be real about how likely that is. A stalker, maybe? He could be trying to case the place."

It is also possible that this mystery man is one of the Forgotten.

Damn. This mess was getting worse by the second. "We need to figure out exactly where Monk is staying so we can protect him."

"Doesn't he have his own people for that?"

"It really depends on what he's dealing with." I knew for a fact that Silas Monk would have been utterly destroyed by any of the vampires I had to kill. And I had a strong suspicion that this new interloper was not on his appointment schedule.

"I'll take your word for that." Namiko brought a photo up on her phone. "Here's a shot of him outside a hotel in Palo Alto. I'm pretty sure it's the Onyx. That's probably where he's staying."

I rolled my eyes. "I can't even afford to dream about that place." But even as the words left my mouth, I knew I'd have to get in somehow.

When I looked the place up online, the idea of infiltrating the hotel seemed impossible. Not only did it have tight security for super wealthy, famous people, but it was also tall as hell.

"He couldn't pick a place that's like three stories high with parking lot access?" I grumbled. "It's gotta be the Everest of luxury hotels, and I'm willing to bet money he's on the top floor."

I still wanted to speak with Monk, but the odds were looking worse by the second. Namiko stood up.

"Take this." She dropped a device that looked like a tiny bean in my palm. "It's an earpiece. So I can help you. When I get home, I'm going to see if I can send you some stuff that'll make your job a lot easier. Watch your phone in like, half an hour." Without waiting for an answer, she pulled up her scarf and slipped out the door. I peeked through the curtain to see the silver sedan make its escape.

"Do you trust her?" I asked Marcus nonchalantly. A layer of drowsiness threatened to descend on me again. I leaned back on the hotel pillows.

It appears that we have no choice. While my faith in you is unerring, the structure where Monk presently resides would be a fool's errand for one person to handle alone. If Namiko offers her aid, we must accept or run a much greater risk of failure that we cannot afford. Do you disagree?

I shook my head. "Nope. Just making sure it wasn't just me."

Right before noon, my phone shook me out of a daze with a message from Namiko: **Put in your earpiece**.

I did as instructed. Within seconds, I could hear yet another voice in my ear. My head was getting awfully crowded.

"Vic? Testing."

"You're good," I said. "Loud and clear."

"I found some maps that might be helpful to you. They're basically just floor plans, but at least this way you'll sort of know where you're going. Obviously, when we're done with this you should delete them, just in case."

"Whatever you say, Namiko."

"Great. It's not much, and you're going to have to improvise, but you're good at that, right? If you leave now, you'll get there in about thirty-five minutes, give or take a few. Oh, and you were right—Monk is king of the hill. Right at the top. And I'm positive the place is full of security, if only because he's there."

I allowed myself no more than a brief moment of self-pity, and then it was time to get ready for the show. Ten minutes later, my Uber driver pulled out onto the road heading south toward Palo Alto.

As I rode, I tried to think of ways to tell a very rich man that he was in mortal danger.

"OH, DAMMIT," Namiko mumbled through the earpiece. "I have some good news and some bad news."

"Good news first," I replied.

"A friend owed me a favor. He has the cameras from the Onyx streaming to my machine as we speak. I've got a god's eye view of the place."

"Funny." I paused on my approach toward the ground floor of the Onyx. "What's the bad news?"

"Remember how I said the place is probably full of security? That wasn't an exaggeration. Be careful. I don't know what they're packing."

"I'll do my best," I said. "Can I bypass the ones on the bottom?"

"Yeah. Go straight through the lobby to the elevators. There's one that goes directly to the top, but it's not available to the general public. You'll need to get off on the level below and find a way up."

"And I'm guessing there will be guards there, too."

"You got it," she confirmed.

This was going to be a regular freakin' riot.

16

THE ONYX HAD THIRTY FLOORS, the topmost of which was reserved for the likes of Silas Monk. I sauntered casually across the lobby and front desk security and stepped into an open elevator as if I were a rich person who belonged in here.

Thumbing the button for floor twenty-nine, I clasped my hands in front of me and stood quietly for the smooth and silent ride up, jazz piping through the elevator speakers. The doors opened on a lushly carpeted hallway where sound seemed to stop in its tracks before ever reaching the other end.

I saw the first guard's shadow on the silk floral wallpaper immediately upon exiting the elevator car.

"Only one," Namiko said. "Move fast. The others will be coming back around."

I crouched slightly, pinned my body to the wall, and crept up behind the guard as he stood innocently keeping watch. I struck silently, and my new strength allowed me to let his unconscious bulk down gently to the floor.

"Okay, get ready to do that four more times," Namiko said like it was no big deal.

I stepped over him, shaking my hands out. "Are they all going to be coming down this way?"

"Yep. Just make sure you get them all so you have the maximum amount of time before someone figures out that something's wrong."

"Roger."

So, I waited in that corridor, put the first two guys in chokeholds, and hit the last two neatly over the head. I left them sleeping peacefully where they fell.

"What am I looking for, now? Stairs?"

"I think so. There should be a stairwell right around—"

"Hey! What are you doing up here?"

I looked toward the owner of the voice—a surprise sixth guard—and then booked it in the opposite direction, hoping he wouldn't immediately radio for help. He didn't, which was gratifying. Even more gratifying was spotting an open room door with a housecleaning cart in front of it. Spinning the cart horizontally to block his path, I grabbed the heavy mop from its holder on the side and used it to whack my pursuer from a distance. He crashed to the muffling carpet, out cold.

I glanced around. "The good news is that I don't see the cleaning lady anywhere, so I don't have to attack an inno-cent woman. The bad news: all the doors I'm seeing are marked with alarm signs. There might be one or two that don't set it off, but I'm not willing to risk it."

"That *is* a problem," Namiko said. She lapsed into focused silence.

"Wait." I peered into an open room at the sliding glass door leading to the balcony. "I have an idea. A really, really shitty idea. Stand by."

The glass opened without a sound to admit me onto the balcony. This high up, the wind tossed my hair, threatening to pull out my loose ponytail. I looked directly upward. The bottom of the top floor's extended balcony hung above me.

Bingo.

I grabbed a chair from the room and dragged it outside. I tested my weight with one foot, and it seemed sturdy enough. I climbed onto the seat cushion and swung my arms a little, preparing for the highest vertical leap I could muster.

"Oh man, this is such a bad idea. In the running for the worst I've ever had." I couldn't help but laugh a little at myself, even as I swayed in the open air. "Necessity is the mother of insanity."

I believe that phrase has been altered, Marcus remarked. *But fear not, Victoria. This is hardly the most foolhardy thing I have ever seen. There was one time in Rome when—*

"Dude, don't get me wrong. I definitely love every single story you've ever told me, but I need to concentrate right now. If I miss this, I'm in some serious shit."

"What was that, Vic?" Namiko asked in my ear.

I almost laughed out loud. I forgot she could hear every word, even the ones that I said to the centuries-old centurion hanging around my neck. "Nothing. Just...um... talking to myself." She didn't respond.

The wind buffeted me mercilessly. Before Marcus or Namiko could start talking again, I jumped.

The tips of my fingers just brushed the iron underbars of the balcony foundation, but I couldn't quite secure my grip. When I came back down, my balance faltered on the chair's plush seat, and I almost busted my ass on the floor. "Oh, shit!"

"What's going on?" Namiko asked, alarmed.

I sucked in my breath. "Don't worry about it. I'm fine." The heartbeat jackhammering crazily in my chest suggested otherwise, but she couldn't hear it, and I wasn't telling her.

The second time, I bent my knees slightly and jumped when the wind wasn't blowing as strong. My left hand ended up flailing in empty air, but the right caught hold of a metal rod. Half gasping with breathless, pounding adrenaline, I began to monkey-bar my way across the balcony supports until I reached the outer side where the railing was. My hand barely fit over the lip of the balcony floor, but barely was enough.

"Where are you?" Namiko asked. "It's so loud."

I didn't answer, only because I was too busy making sure I didn't fall to my death. Once I had a firm hold on the iron struts, I hoisted myself up and over the top. Then I lay there for a minute, still gasping and trying not to think about what I'd just done. If anything had gone wrong, I would have died outright. Not my wisest, most well thought out plan, but effective and fun, in a terrifying way.

"Okay," I told Namiko finally. "I'm on the balcony. The top balcony."

"You're what?! How did you get there?"

"Up and over. Took the scenic route." I was on my feet again, stretching the nervous tremors from my legs.

"That seems rather foolish," she said calmly. Now that her initial surprise had worn off, she sounded like a long-suffering parent admonishing an idiot child.

I chose to ignore it. "It wasn't so bad. Now what?"

"The top balcony wraps all the way around to the front entrance of the thirtieth-floor suite. Just follow it until you see another door."

The wind still tugged playfully at my clothes, though its strength was far less threatening with my feet on solid ground. My hair was a wild mess of tangles, the tie forever lost to the void. On the opposite side of the building, the gale died down, and I was able to smooth my mane into something halfway presentable as I walked up to the entrance leading into the suite.

"I'm here," I told Namiko. "Should I just…"

Silence. I felt around inside my ear for that little bean, but it was gone. Another casualty of the cruel winds.

Alone now, I reached out and tried the door. It swung open into a room with another set of doors. Through the glass, I could see a lamp on in a back room. My brain spun into overdrive; I still hadn't figured out what I wanted to say.

After a moment's uncertain pause, I just whispered, "Whatever," under my breath, raised my hand, and knocked.

Footsteps came toward the door. The lock disengaged. The knob turned.

Eve stood on the threshold, smiling. She wasn't wearing the blood red ensemble from the gala, and her hair was down around her shoulders. I might have believed she was normal, except for those piercing eyes.

"Hello, Victoria," she sang, seemingly unsurprised to see me. "Please come in." She let the door shut behind me. "You look like you've been stuck out in the weather, poor thing. What can I do for you?"

I took a deep breath. "Well, I realized earlier that I never got a chance to talk directly with Mr. Monk, so I thought it couldn't hurt to drop by and try again."

"Oh, of course, sweetheart. I'm sorry. That's probably all my fault. You're just so interesting, I had to keep you all to myself."

Just then, another door swung open in the back of the suite. "Eve?" Silas Monk emerged from what I assumed to be a bedroom. We looked at each other with equal bewilderment.

"Eve!" Monk said. "You can't just let strangers into the room like this! This is my home right now. My private sanctuary!" He turned to me. "How did you get up here, anyway? I thought I had the elevator sealed to the public."

I shrugged. "Sorry, sir." It was all I could think to say. The awkward silence that descended was thick enough to be palpable.

"Be calm, Silas." Eve focused her radiant blue eyes on him. "Everything is all right. There's nothing to get upset about. She just wants to talk to you."

As Eve spoke, the air in the room grew softer—I could feel it caressing my skin. Monk settled more or less immediately. He adjusted his shirt's fit, brushing off the collar and cuffs. "I hope you'll forgive me," he said, sounding much more like his normal, easily confident self. "I've been under a lot of stress these past few days." He examined me closer. "You were at last night's reveal, weren't you?"

I nodded. "It was an incredible honor to witness the unveiling of your latest masterpiece." Laying it on a little thick, but I knew Monk's type. Guys like him loved to have their egos stroked; craved it, even. He made a big show of waving away the compliment, even as his chest puffed out.

"Please, you're too kind." He made a grand, sweeping gesture toward the sitting room. "Why don't we use the furniture like civilized people?" The coffee table had a full, untouched service on it. "Feel free to help yourself to anything you like." Monk sat back on the couch cushions. "Really, it's no trouble. I don't think I caught your name, Miss...?"

"Vic. Just Vic is fine."

Monk stroked his chin. "I like that. It suits you." He scooted over to make room for Eve, who lowered herself elegantly down beside him. "And I have to say, I admire the ingenuity it must have taken to find a way up here."

Eve chortled. "That's why I let her in, *love*. I think you two would get along just perfectly."

"You're never wrong, my darling." Monk leaned over and planted a kiss on the woman's cheek. "So, what is it that you're so keen to discuss with me?"

I had expected my nerves to get worse as the conversation went on, but I noticed, looking between the two of them, that I was perfectly at ease. Eve's gentle smile and Monk's laid-back demeanor dissolved all the pressure I had put on myself on the way up. "I'm interested in the LIGHT drill as a multifunctional device." At least half that sentence had been completely bullshitted up, but Monk didn't seem to mind.

"You mean as a weapon," he said, cutting right to the heart of the matter. "I've never denied the possibility of LIGHT arms being developed, either right now or sometime in the future. And of course, it's important to emphasize that I'm not what you'd call a warmonger. Not at all. But we need to be able to keep up with the advance of technology around the globe. We're not the only country constantly seeking to innovate and improve. If we want to maintain our position as one of the tech industry's global leaders, it's important for us to explore all avenues, including those that may be viewed as controversial."

Spoken like a true salesman. I smiled and got ready to burst his bubble.

"What's the likelihood that the LIGHT drill might end up in the wrong hands?"

Be careful, Victoria.

Marcus's warning barely registered over the gentle buzzing filling the room. Or was it filling my mind? I couldn't be sure.

Briefly, Monk was shocked. He laughed as he recovered himself and said, "Right now, the drill is only equipped to be used as a gamechanger in the energy industry. It is also the only prototype to have successfully completed production, so we're not treating weaponization as a primary concern. We don't know of anyone who would want to use the drill for anything other than its specific, marketed purpose."

I tilted my head to the side. "You don't? Because I do."

Victoria. Be mindful of your words.

Marcus's voice was stronger this time, urgent. But I just didn't care. Silas and Eve were there to listen to me, to understand my concerns. For some reason, I knew that with certainty. And as a creator of potential weapons himself, Silas deserved to know what darkness was lurking in the world.

"Please do enlighten me," Monk said. His casual posture disappeared; he sat forward and ready, a spark of hungry intellect alight in his eye. Eve still reclined against the sofa, fondly stroking his shoulder.

"Vampires," I said.

No!

"What was that?" he asked.

"You heard me," I said.

He nodded, and the gears in Monk's formidable brain began to turn. "But what do you mean by that?"

"Real ones. Created from the blood of a god. I've seen them being manufactured. Mass produced." The words came out easily.

Victoria, stop! You don't know what you're saying!

Marcus's voice was like a mosquito whining constantly in my ear. I pulled off the medallion and stuck it in my pocket. This was just one more thing he would never understand. If Monk knew everything, he could help us, and we would win the inevitable war.

Monk's eyes narrowed. "Gods, you say? And you mean the kind I think you mean? Omniscient, all powerful, each governing separate domains? I'm going to need proof of that."

"I have some."

I reached into my bag and grasped the sword hilt. Eve's

eyes went wide enough that I knew she understood exactly what it was. Monk, on the other hand, was less impressed.

"How do I know that's not just a weird, useless artifact?"

"Because." I stood up and stepped away from the very flammable couch. "This is what it does."

The astonishment etched on Silas Monk's face upon beholding the *Gladius Solis* for the first time legitimately warmed my soul. I was proud to have shared something new with a man whose hands created so much. For a minute after I extinguished the blade, he stared speechless at the hilt.

"How did you..." He shook his head. "I feel like my entire world has just been shifted."

"Darling." Eve reached out a slender hand and took mine. "That sword is a sacred object with a myriad of undiscovered properties. Who knows what miracles are hiding within its golden blade? You must entrust it to us so that Silas may study it further and use its strength to better humankind."

The medallion burned in my pocket. I looked between Eve and Kronin's sword, and then between Silas Monk and the sword. Eve was right; if Monk applied his brand of genius to the power of the *Gladius Solis*, he could do incredible, revolutionary things. He was a far greater hero than I was, that was suddenly clear to me.

This was a gift I owed to the world and one I was willing to give to them.

"Take good care of it," I said to Eve. "Please. It's way more important than I have time to explain." There was no denying her words.

I reached out my hand to give her the sword.

But before she could reach it, the room descended into chaos.

The window overlooking the city skyline shattered into thousands of tiny shards. A cool breeze filled the room, and I felt very strange. As if I was waking up from a dream. Eve shrieked and recoiled; the hilt dropped to the floor. A long, sharp object whistled through the gaping maw in the glass. I ducked to the side. "What the hell!"

Another shriek cracked the air. I noticed drops of crimson pooling on the floor, leading up to Eve hunched over with her hands on the knife in her side. I grabbed for the hilt and tried to scramble to her, but a massive weight came down in front of me, obscuring her from my view.

"Hey!" I cried. "Who the fuck are you?"

"Stay out of this." The voice resonated deeper than any other I'd ever heard, underscored by a touch of gravel. A pixie dusting of glass was still raining down on everything, lending a glittering haze to the unknown figure. He hefted a vicious-looking hammer above Eve's prone body. The voice sounded again.

"This is my fight."

His fight?

"Like hell it is!"

I stumbled to my feet, still trying to figure out what the shit just went down. The newcomer stood with his heavy-ass hammer poised above Eve, looking down at her. "Reveal yourself, creature," he said. "Your kind is nothing more than lies."

"Marcus, who is this, and what the hell is he talking about?" Remembering myself, I put the medallion over my head.

Vic, you are out of your depth here. You need to leave, now.

"What? He's gonna kill Eve!"

I very much doubt that he will.

Unconvinced, I started toward her body, which was now stained with blood. Two steps in, she twitched and rolled over, moaning. The knife dislodged from her slide and clattered onto the tiled floor. Eve took a slow, deep breath.

The blood stopped.

She rolled again, gathering her limbs beneath her and using them to push up onto her hands and knees. Her golden hair fell forward as she arched her neck down.

A sharp hissing began to come from somewhere, but it wasn't until her head snapped back up that I realized the sound was coming from between her bared teeth. The shoulders of her blouse burst outward in a rain of shredded fabric, destroyed by the emergence of two giant wings.

"Okay, I need to ask a question," I said. "What in seven hells is that?"

Eve was standing now, the tips of her wings almost dragging on the floor. The corpses of her blouse and skirt clung to her changed body, and when she looked at me now, it was with wide, burning, hate-filled eyes.

But I wasn't the one with whom she had a bone to pick.

"*You!*" Eve brandished a skinny, almost skeletal finger, tipped with a long, sharp nail, in the direction of the hammer guy. "Intruder! The weapons are for our hands only, not for your kind of vermin!"

"My kind of vermin? Lady, have you seen yourself lately?" He lifted his hands and began to whip the hammer in lazy circles around his head. "You're in no position to be throwing that term around."

She flew at him, kicking up a storm of debris with her massive wings. "Get out! Go back to Hell and stay there!"

The man laughed. "I get that a lot. Never seems to take, though."

"I don't know whose side I'm supposed to be on," I murmured.

It is safe to assume that neither is ideal at the moment. Choose the side of the living.

The hammer picked up speed, blurring into one oblong shape in the air. Its wielder maintained the same stoic expression.

"Come any closer, and I'll roast you alive, you damn vulture." He showed no signs of tiring or wanting to slow down, and the effective barrier created by his weapon only served to enrage Eve more. I could just glimpse Silas Monk crouching behind the relative safety of a solid wooden side runner at her back. His face seemed to have set permanently in a mask of confused shock and horror.

I was past the horror part, but confusion and shock still got me, especially since Marcus was in the same boat. We retreated farther into the sitting room where there were no windows to shatter on us.

"You really don't know what's going on?" I eyed the standoff between Hammer Guy and Eve, my rat's nest of hair getting extra tangled by the drafts from her wings. "Like, are they gonna each land one major strike that cancel each other out and explode? I would rather not be here when that happens."

I'm unsure of who he is, but it's clear now what we've been dealing with. Eve is a harpy—and the red-headed female from the warehouse was probably one as well.

I made a face. "Well harpies look freaking gross." It was like all her skin had simultaneously stretched and aged across her body. The teeth behind her faded red lips were needlelike and jagged, and when she opened her mouth all the way, her jaw gaped wide. To me, she was a child's nightmare drawing come to life.

Not only are they formidable fighters, they have power over the mind.

"What, like they can make someone bark like a dog and roll over?"

Like she could make you ignore me—your loving and trusted advisor. But worse, she could make you give her the Gladius Solis. Kronin's blade and the one weapon we have against the coming darkness.

"What? There's no way she could…" But then I looked down at the hilt in my hand, and a sense of horror came over me as the realization hit of what I had almost done.

"Oh, shit."

Indeed. Now if you're done flirting with the bird-woman, I suggest we depart. This room is about to become a warzone.

I looked up at Eve and saw her crouching, guarded before the large man. It was clear he knew how to handle himself, but beyond that I couldn't get a read on him.

It was like he was determined not to look like anything or anyone. He made me think of Namiko in a way, with his thick, black glasses and gloves and trench coat that touched the floor. The antithesis to the harpy's neurotic, constant movement in every way, he manipulated the hammer as though it weighed nothing, calmly waiting for the perfect moment to strike.

They sustained this terrible harmony for a couple of minutes longer until Eve's wild impatience boiled over. With a head-splitting war cry, she fanned out her wings and rushed him again, aiming to claw out one or more of his vital organs.

The man in the shades didn't flinch. He simply spun his hammer faster until fire erupted along the iron face. The flames were orange, then blue, then white in rapid succession. By the time Eve realized she was on a direct collision course with his controlled meteor, it was too late.

The impact made a horrible sizzle that awoke the last remaining dregs of my squeamishness and forced me to look away. Somewhere beneath her agonized screaming, I thought I picked out the sound of vomiting too, courtesy of Silas Monk.

Funny how quickly the glamor had been torn right out of his life.

But Eve was far from dead. The harpy's haggard silhouette stood out against the flames from the hammer, one shaking limb jabbed toward the enemy.

"Look at what you've done!" she howled. "Look at my face! My beautiful, exquisite, precious face!"

"Trust me," said the hammer man. "I've seen it, and it's none of those things now."

I braced myself for another wild rage, but she sank to the floor, clutching her face and sobbing with her whole body. Seizing the opportunity, I ran behind her and grabbed hold of her former lover.

"Come on, Monk. We have to go!" He was slow to regain his sense of motion, but he followed along without complaint once I'd gotten him to his feet. "Does the elevator work?"

"Huh? Yeah, for me." He pulled a cardkey from his pocket.

"Well, start that thing up before he decides to come after us."

On cue, that deep voice roared, "Oh no you don't. You're not getting away, technician!"

The cardkey slid into the reader, and we both got a face-full of angry, charging hammer before the doors slammed shut just in time.

But the elevator didn't move. The sides of the doors began to dimple. Hammer Man was holding it in place just to keep Monk from escaping. I reached down into my bag.

This was a scenario that called for the big guns.

The *Gladius Solis* stabbed straight through the elevator doors the same way it cut through everything else: as if it were paper. I heard the guy on the other side give a wary grunt, and the elevator car was released. Silas immediately reached for the button panel. I stopped him.

"Wait. I want to try something." The car wavered back into place, waiting for an input, and I put my thumb to the Door Open button.

"What are you doing?! Are you crazy? He's gonna come rushing at us as soon as he sees the doors start to go!" Silas's face was pale and clammy. He had never looked less like a billionaire playboy.

"That's what I want! As long as your reflexes are good enough." The elevator opened to reveal our friend had backed up to the other side of the room, getting a good running start. Exactly as I'd expected. "Okay Monk, go when I say go." I waited for four tense seconds, judging the distance as our adversary charged forward. "Go!"

We exploded from the elevator, and on my way out, I swung the *Gladius Solis* up to the farthest extent of its reach so that it just managed to slice through the elevator ceiling and fatally wound the car's main support cable. Unable to slow his momentum in time, Hammer Guy smashed into the back of the open car, which rocked, wavered unsteadily, before the cables snapped.

Its passenger roared all the way down.

"Shit, that was the elevator!" Monk cried. "Now what do we do?"

I gave him a look. "Now we take the stairs."

That was easier said than done. The door I chose happened to be rigged with an alarm, which blared so loudly I couldn't hear myself think. Still, it was our only option, and after the elevator crashed down into the lobby, an alarm didn't seem out of place.

So, I grabbed the genius inventor with one hand, my sword in the other, and started running. The first few floors were okay, but the lower we got, the more wholesale panic we encountered; not to mention that some congestion was caused by two newly-arriving harpies in cocktail dresses coming up to meet us instead of the other way around. These ladies had their wings out, blocking the path with armatures of feather and bone. I felt Monk balk at the sight of them.

"This is not happening," he mumbled, somewhat maniacally. "Not happening. Not happening."

"Stay with me, Monk. We have to get through this together!" It was the nice way of saying he was too important to leave his ass behind.

The stairwells were too narrow and crowded to use the blade, so I resorted to bludgeoning via hilt, and also good, old-fashioned shoving. This was when I discovered that the harpies were built like brick shithouses under all that blinding, ethereal beauty. As I tried to barrel my way past them, they squared up between the railing and the wall, their wings bristling. Claws tore at my hair and clothes.

Monk screamed. I could tell he was really losing it. "No!" he shouted." Get...get away from me! Get the hell away from me!"

One of the harpies, in direct defiance of his request, thrust her arm over my shoulder in an attempt to grab him. It was a greedy mistake. I seized her forearm, used it to wrench her off balance. The bulk of her wings, formerly a formidable hindrance, now worked against her. I dropped down as she fell forward, driving my shoulder up into her chest. She struck the railing hard, flailing against me. I took a couple serious wallops to the head and shoulders. A hank of my hair came out in her fist.

"Oh, screw you!" I shouted. "That fucking hurts!" Her friend rushed forward, and I braced myself against the steps, shoving with all my might. The harpy's center of gravity tipped. There was something infinitely satisfying about the wretched screening sound she made as she plummeted down to the first floor.

I wished I could say for his sake that Silas Monk was dashing and helpful, but he wasn't. He mostly used me as a human shield, which I could hardly blame him for, since I was the one with the sword. This strategy became slightly less effective when the hotel security started flooding up the steps. I almost lost him a couple times just because he couldn't follow up after I'd whipped a harpy or strong-armed a guard out of his way.

At least he wasn't crying. Or getting sick anymore.

The first-floor stairwell had two possible exits: one that led into the lobby and one that emptied into the underground parking garage. I grabbed Monk's elbow. "You got a car in there?"

He nodded, apparently devoid of words as this point.

"Is it fast?" I asked. He nodded again. "Good enough! Let's go."

And that was how Silas Monk and I ended up leading a caravan of uniformed security personnel, monster harpies thinly disguised as gorgeous women, and the occasional, very confused luxury hotel guest on a conga line of madness through the Onyx subterranean lot.

If nothing else, I was learning to find fun in the strangest places. Plus, Monk's car turned out to be a banana-yellow Aston Martin convertible, which would undoubtedly kill us both instantly if we got into an accident.

So, I made him put the top down.

I was determined to die in style.

Monk, who'd been catatonic for at least ten minutes by the time we found his car, came back to himself enough to insist that he had to be the driver. He yanked the top down in a heartbeat, and as his car careened wildly over the brushed-stone paths of the garage, I leaned out the passenger's side and clubbed anyone who didn't get out of the way in time.

I'd be lying if I said it wasn't fun as hell.

Well, it was fun until Monk nearly decapitated us going underneath the gate to leave the garage. I could have sworn the lady in the ticket window fainted as I ducked to keep the stick from coming down on my neck. He whipped out to the right, and we burned down the street, ahead of a wave of sirens and flashing lights.

I glanced over my shoulder. "Hope you're a good driver, Monk!"

"Are you kidding me?" A grim smile broke across his features. "Who do you think you're talking to?"

"A nerd," I said.

"Not just any nerd. A nerd with money out the ass!" Spotting a police cruiser coming at us from a side street, Silas punched the gas. The car leapt forward, clearing the police bumper by a scant few inches. He whooped as we left it in the dust.

"You should've told me all it would take to cheer you up is to let you almost destroy us both in a flashy car," I said as I gripped the armrest.

"Hey, I am not almost destroying us. I know exactly what I'm—"

His bragging was cut short by a huge thud and then a frantic shout. At first, I thought we'd hit a large black dog, and my stomach sank with the guilt. Then I saw the glint of eyes behind a thick curtain of hair. The harpy's claws dug into the yellow hood, and it snarled at Monk and me. This one looked particularly feral.

Monk began to spin the wheel furiously. "What are you *doing?*" I yelled, over the squealing tires.

"Trying to shake her off! She's wrecking the paint!"

I glared. My shoulder slammed into the top of his car door. "Ow, dammit! If you don't cut that ego trip and drive, I'm gonna knock you out and take the wheel. Understood?"

"Yes, ma'am." He took the next right way too hard, and even though I almost fell out of the car, our little hitch-hiker actually did fall off, so it was worth it.

Monk zipped down some side streets for a while, winding among houses with trees in the front and playgrounds in the back. The sound of sirens faded in the distance, but as soon as we shot out onto another main road, the cops resumed the chase. But as it turned out, Silas Monk was more than happy to drive his snazzy yellow Aston Martin like a total asshole.

I cringed every time he squeezed narrowly between two cars or took an exit ramp at ninety miles an hour. We made more U-turns than I could count.

If I didn't think about the fact that there was a man out there probably hunting us like animals so he could settle a score with Silas Monk—whatever that score happened to be—riding in a fast car with a billionaire almost made me forget about my troubles in the thirty seconds between cop sightings.

"Nice car!" I shouted over the squealing tires.

"Yeah, but we should have taken the Hummer," he answered. "Then we could have just run them over."

Hard to argue with that logic. "I'll remind you next time."

After forty minutes of speeding back and forth all over the city, tracing and retracing our tracks, Monk just narrowly avoided a miniature jam getting onto the freeway that cut off our pursuers. Monk cheered as we sailed ahead into the middle lane.

"Hold on," I said. "You know this isn't over, right? Now you need to tell me what's going on with you so I know how deep this goes."

"What do you mean, how deep? I made a drill that will save Earth huge energy costs in the long run. Things didn't get weird until I met Eve." He went quiet for a moment. "I can't believe that guy hit her with a flaming *fucking* hammer."

"Did you not see her transform into a horrible creature of myth right before that?" I sort of couldn't believe this guy.

He was under her spell, Marcus said.

That made a lot more sense.

"She… transformed?" Monk looked horrified and a little sick all at once. "I don't remember… wait… I do remember *them* turning into monsters. Holy shit!" His hand tightened and released on the wheel, knuckles whitening. "Shit. Those weren't just nightmares. Shit, shit, shit." He started to lose the color in his lips. "I don't feel so good, man. It's like, I thought those were just dreams, or episodes, or something. I thought I wasn't really there. Oh, man."

"Do you need to pull over and puke on your shoes?" I had my left arm ready to grab the steering wheel in case he passed out. "Cause if not, this sounds like a story I really want to hear. For more reasons than one."

"Yeah, all right." He tried his best to take some deep breaths, calm the persistent shaking in his hands. "Look, I'm not that hungry, but maybe…maybe it would be better if we stopped somewhere for a second. Just real quick." He kept his gaze fixed on the road, as if he thought looking anywhere else would jeopardize his grip on reality. "I need a minute to process all this bullshit."

"Fine by me. I'm starving." I was also worried about having him behind the wheel. He'd gotten kind of a wild, unpredictable look in his eye. "Take the next exit. I don't care what's there."

Monk pulled into an old-fashioned burger joint on the

side of the road, gave me some money, and we ate in the car while he told me how he'd gotten mixed up in this mess.

"Honestly, I can't remember exactly where I met Eve. It was sort of like she just appeared one day, and we were suddenly inseparable. A lot of the details are fuzzy in hindsight, and it makes me wonder what was going on during those times."

Mind control, said Marcus. *Quite effective, as far as I can fathom. The harpy's secret weapon.*

I decided to keep that fact to myself. No use freaking Monk out even further when we still had to drive back to San Francisco. He was away from Eve for now, but she wasn't dead yet. We would have to go back to finish her off.

"What's going to happen to her?" he asked, intruding almost uncannily on my thoughts. "I know what you think you saw—what I think I saw—but I'm not...it's just not fucking possible. It's not possible!"

I forced myself to have patience with this guy, maybe even a little sympathy. In the span of a few short hours, he'd had his charmed-ass life thrown into total upheaval. "Which part?" I asked slowly. "Because I hate to tell you this, but it's all possible, and it's all happening. To you. Right now."

"She's not a harpy." Monk sounded angry now, and I guessed I couldn't blame him. From his perspective, I was little more than a vehicle of slander against his hot lady friend. "Harpies don't exist! This is ludicrous!"

"I'll give you that last part," I said. "About this being ludicrous. But that's it."

"Shit," he muttered. He was still holding onto the wheel with one hand. His face was red. I had to calm him down before he just dropped dead from stress and denial.

"I'm not saying this isn't tough, or that it doesn't suck balls. Trust me, I know. But like I said, it's happening, and we don't have that much time. The best thing we can do now is move forward. Which means I need you to help me try to figure things out. At least this way you're being proactive, right?"

At first, I got nothing. Then his shoulders started to slump, the tension leaking out of his body. He leaned back in the driver's seat and shut his eyes. "Yeah." He spoke almost gently. "Yeah. You're right." The inventor's chest rose and fell. "Go ahead, then."

"When did you start working with her?" I asked, feeling like an interrogator with a jumpy witness. I couldn't lose him until I figured out what the hell the gods thought they were doing, screwing around with a new weapon. And I knew we might need him in the event that we'd have to use the drill in self-defense. Who better to explain how to use it than its inventor?

"It wasn't until after the production prototype was finalized. Eve came on to me strong, started talking about not getting younger and how that really made her passionate about the planet's future. All the right stuff, basically. The stuff I want to hear. She told me she had extremely generous investors who couldn't put a price on innovation. I should have known it was too good to be true. But I let it slide until the first investors' meeting. That was when I met *her*."

Ah yes, her.

I couldn't decide if it was good or bad that Marcus already knew who Silas was talking about.

"Eve blindfolded me for the ride to the meeting place, which was not *completely* usual for business meetings, but I mean, I've been called quirky a million times over the course of my career. If they wanted to keep their location under wraps, who was I to argue? And I was extremely gung ho about this project myself, so honestly, I would have let them get away with almost anything." He frowned. "I think Eve must have known that.

"So, they brought me into this room, sat me down in this chair, and took the blindfold off. And at first, there was just an empty chair there that's obviously nicer than the one they gave me. I was thinking I'd gotten conned, and I was trying to formulate a plan to get out of there. But they finally bring in the person they say is 'the investor.'" He paused to experience the memory to its fullest extent. "She's unlike anything I've ever seen. To be honest, it's difficult to picture her clearly. But she was an amazingly gorgeous woman, and she made me...certain promises—as long as I told her about the drill."

"You didn't think that was weird?" I asked. He really was the perfect target for a pack of power hungry harpies: dreamy, idealistic, wickedly smart, and yet still able to get shit done.

"You know what I thought was weird?" Monk asked. "This woman was like, nine feet tall. Even now, I don't really know if that's right or if it's something I made up. I just recall her towering over everyone else. Maybe that one thing was enough to make everything else seem normal by comparison." He shook his head. "I don't know. I really don't know. And I don't say that a lot."

Her name is Lysiani. She is a goddess and the master of seduction. Tell the scientist that.

I hesitated. Silas Monk was in a fragile state at the moment, maybe one of the most fragile states of his life. Could his extremely secular world withstand the blow of learning that gods were real? What if his head exploded? What if he flipped out and crashed the car?

If he is to help protect the weapon he has built, he must know about the Forgotten and the true threat they pose. And you had no qualms about revealing this truth to him earlier.

I cleared my throat. "Monk? I need to tell you something that's gonna make a lot of sense and none at all, at the same time." He didn't say anything, but his eyes caught mine, which I took as clearance to proceed. "She was nine feet tall because she's *actually* a goddess named Lysiani."

"A goddess," he said, his blank eyes fixed on the floorboards at his feet. "What would a goddess want with a geothermal mining tool?"

For all intents and purposes, I had temporarily ceased to exist. His brain required every inch of space it could find to try and make space for the possibility of this new truth. Convincing a "normal" person of the Forgotten was hard enough, a scientist would take some work. Thankfully, he'd seen some *really* strange shit lately.

I gave him a nudge in the right direction. "Nothing, dude. That's why I asked about weaponization."

Okay, so it was less a nudge and more of an impatient shove, but I knew what was at stake better than he did, and while I was totally sympathetic to his maelstrom of feelings, we didn't really have time to discuss them in a burger joint parking lot on the side of the highway.

"It has a laser in it," Monk said numbly. "Everything I said back at the hotel is still true. The laser isn't a weapon, but it could be." He closed his eyes. "I think she told me what she wanted to do with it. I just... didn't want to hear."

"Was it something about killing gods?" I asked. Then I said, "How about we swap seats? You can drool over this all you want as a passenger. I got shit to do."

All the fuss had gone out of him. We switched places, and he settled back as I started the engine. "So, is that what it takes to kill a god-level being?"

"What do you mean?" I asked.

"I designed that drill from the ground up. I know exactly what it's capable of. And you're telling me it would be enough to kill a god?" A wry smile emerged on his lips. "I should be proud of that, shouldn't I?"

"Depends on who has control of the drill."

"Uh oh," Monk said.

"What? You never thought of that?"

He pointed through the window of the burger joint at the anachronistically large TV mounted on the wall inside. "Isn't that you?"

The freeze frame of my face took up most of the screen. It had been ripped from hotel security footage, so the image wasn't as clear as it could have been. I squinted. Monk only knew it was me because he was involved. The security camera was far too grainy to give anyone a positive ID on me.

"Yeah it is," I said. "And we gotta get the hell out of here. I'll give you that. Not your biggest problem, though."

"Which would be what? That some nine-foot-tall goddess wants to use the tech I've practically gifted her to take over the world?"

"Not even." I turned out of the lot and put the gas pedal to the floor. "If they've got me on tape, then they have you, too."

I ONLY DROVE the Aston Martin for ten minutes before ditching it on some quiet side street in favor of a less conspicuous car. "Just buy another one after this all blows over," I told Monk. "Or like… buy it back from the police. You're rich; can't you do that?"

"No." He sighed. "Well, maybe."

"See? Problem solved."

The nondescript grey hatchback I chose coughed to life, and I took it the long way back to the freeway just in case we'd been followed somehow. Even away from the city center, the alleyways were slanted and narrow. I was navigating purely on instinct, hoping none of my turns would result in a dead end.

That luck held out for longer than I expected, but not long enough to keep us out of trouble.

"There's no outlet," Monk said. "Oh shit, it's the guy from the hotel!"

He stood dead center in the alley, still looking like a dystopian sci-fi extra in trench coat and glasses, still wearing a big-ass hammer across his back. When he saw us, he didn't flee from the path of the oncoming vehicle. He got down into a fighting stance.

Victoria.

"Yeah I see him."

I stepped on the gas.

19

My lead foot lasted only as long as it took for me to realize the dude in the alley wasn't budging. I cursed and stomped on the brake. "Hold on tight!"

The grey hatchback skidded to a hard halt amid the squeal of tires and a cloud of acrid rubber smoke. Silas Monk cowered in the seat beside me, arms over his head. "What the hell is happening?" he demanded, his voice shaky.

"Well, we didn't hit him," I said. "But I think he's about to hit us."

A resounding boom shook the car as his giant hammer slammed the concrete wall next to the car. Debris pattered onto the roof and windshield. The shadow of the weapon passed across the roof and struck again. This time, the debris sounded bigger.

On the next backswing, I flung my door open and rolled low into the alley. Hammer Man beat on the wall a third time, and now I could see it was starting to crumble inward at the point of impact.

"He can't help either of us if you crush him to death," I shouted, standing up and brushing myself off.

"My conflict is not with you, human." He kept his obscured gaze intently on Monk. "It would behoove you to get lost while you still can." He adjusted his grip on the shaft of his hammer, his broad face expressionless beneath those impenetrable sunglasses. His mouth made a hard, dark line beneath a nose that had clearly been broken at least once. With a grunt, he pulled his weapon back for another mighty swing.

"But, see, that's where you're wrong. You've got a beef with Monk, and I need him. So, hell yeah, your conflict *is* with me." The *Gladius Solis* was in my hand now. "Are we gonna sort this shit out or not?"

He stopped mid swing, faltering slightly against his own momentum. "All you're doing is making this worse for yourself."

"Easy is boring." I backed away from the car, hoping he'd take the cue and follow me. "Just one request. Don't blow that thing up, all right? I'm gonna need it to get out of here after I kick your ass."

He laughed gruffly. "It's almost a shame we met this way." Then that damned colossal hammer was coming for my head. I ducked in the nick of time; the edge of it skimmed my hair.

Victoria!

"Not now, Marcus!" I shouted. "In case you haven't noticed, I'm not any less busy than I was a minute ago!"

Kronin's blade sliced through the air, but it clanged to a stop against the shaft of the hammer.

"That's not going to work here," Hammer Guy said smugly. "Guess you'll have to think of a way to ditch the cheat codes."

I was more surprised than I had any right to be, and it pissed me off. Marcus had said over and over again that the sword was unbeatable, and so I felt like I had a right to expect it to actually cut through everything. My first instinct was that this dude had found a way to game the system, even though he called me the cheater.

I braced the flat of the blade against his next strike. Sparks jumped from between the weapons. "Who are you?" I demanded. The sheer weight of the hammer's head gave me the edge I needed. He stepped back, and I forced him up and off. "Come on, spit it out. You're not going to win this, man!"

By way of answering, he swung the hammer up over his head and brought it down two-handed between his feet. A web of rumbling cracks surged toward me, warping the surrounding ground. I leapt out of the way as the shock-wave crashed into the wall at my back.

"Defeat me, and you might be worthy of my name."

"What the shit is *with* you weirdos? You wanna be Hammer Guy for the rest of your life? Fine by me."

Hammer Guy smirked. "I like how you're assuming I'll let you kill me."

I growled. "I'm not assuming shit, dickass. I'm just going to do it."

Victoria, listen to me. Engaging this individual is a mistake.

Back off, retrieve Monk, and get to someplace I can explain without distracting you.

"I don't know, man. I'm already pretty damn engaged." The sword swiped across Hammer Guy's black-clad abdomen as I lunged forward, singeing a hole in his shirt. The fabric stretched as he moved back, and I caught a glimpse of a dark chain-link tattoo on his skin. He responded by jabbing me with the broad end of the hammer. I stumbled back, gasping for breath.

"You got an invisible friend?" Hammer Guy sneered. "Or did Kronin's sword just happen to find its way to a human lunatic this time?" The medallion fell from my neckline as I steadied myself. His eyes snapped to it. "Invisible friend it is." Before I could stop him or get out of reach, he stepped forward and grabbed the chain, inspecting the coat of arms. "I think I know this guy. I'd ask if you killed him, but he probably died saving your life or something. They're all about that shit in Carcerum."

He let go of the medallion, and I stuffed it back into my shirt. "Do me a favor and don't ever touch my shit again." I squared up. "Let's get this over with."

"If you say so." He whipped the hammer down at me, forcing me to dive out of the way. When I looked up, it was already spinning like a rotor above his head. "You were at the hotel before. You know what comes next." The hammer started to sizzle.

"Fuck off!" A torrent of rage burst in my chest, and the next thing I knew, Kronin's sword was flying through the air. Clean throw, but he had too much warning. I watched as he deflected it with the whirring hammer.

Not my finest moment, but I had a trick up my sleeve. I

took a deep breath, held out my hand, and called, "*Gladius Solis!*"

The sword, lying where it had fallen after bouncing off the wall, skidded a few feet in my general direction.

"Not much of a teacher, was he?" Hammer Guy started to advance. "That's all right. He's not here to see this."

The searing heat from the hammer bored down on me, the glare of the fire burning my eyes. I threw myself to the side, barely clearing the white-hot flames, and darted for the sword. The blade came out just in time to save my skull from being forcibly reshaped.

Damn, I wished Monk knew how to fight. Or do anything besides sciency stuff and hiding in a stolen car. Vamps with knives and guns were one thing, but this guy was bigger than Rocco, and his hammer threw me off my game. Plus, it sketched me out that he seemed more interested in treating me like a toy. I'd take pure murderous intent over mind games any day.

"You'll be sorry if he runs," I said. The sword cut upward.

"I'll be surprised if he gets the balls to look out the window." Hammer Guy did a back turn and met my next strike with infuriating ease. "If he runs, I'll go after him. I told you, my conflict isn't with *you.*"

"Aren't I the luckiest girl on Earth?"

"If I'm not mad at you, you're up there." He moved to take another swing but was stopped dead by a screeching cry from the other end of the alley. His head snapped around, and the semi-playful smirk fell off his mouth. "Dammit."

A horde of lithe, slender shapes poured out of the

street, filling the width of the alley like a screaming, vengeful torrent. It took me a second to realize they were harpies. Not as tall as Eve or the other one, but definitely louder.

"Where the hell did they come from?" I asked to no one in particular.

"I've been asking that question my whole life!"

I turned to look at Hammer Guy, but the harpy tide crashed between us, and he was gone behind a wall of wings and slashing claws. The report of the hammer blows cut through the screams with vicious regularity. I could already see the crowd starting to thin.

While the girls were preoccupied with Hammer Guy, I got back to the hatchback, which was now covered in scratches. A skinny hand snatched at me, so I cut it off. The claws clutched grotesquely at nothing.

It almost made me miss the familiarity of my boring New York vamps. Those guys didn't constantly screech like they were on fire. Sure, they catcalled me, but I had established ways of dealing with that.

The door was closed and locked somehow. I could still see Silas Monk scrunched up in the seat. He'd lapsed back into staring silence, but at least he reacted when he noticed me. His thumb hovered over the unlock button on his door panel.

I nodded, and just as I heard the sound of the locks opening, a hand jerked me backward.

The air rushed from my lungs as I landed hard on my back. A short harpy loomed over me. "Going somewhere?" she asked, in a scratchy, witchlike voice. Her skin looked like it had hairline cracks, her eyes bloodshot scarlet. If

Lysiani was the Harpy Queen or whatever, she didn't have very high recruiting standards.

Then again, this bitch had just flung me like a ragdoll, so maybe it was in my best interest not to judge a book by its ratty cover.

She seized me by the arm and hauled me to my feet, aiming to toss me again. I dug the point of my sword into the pavement, stopping her at the cost of a painful jerk to my shoulder. Once she saw what was holding me in place, she bared her teeth, hissing, but she made no move to get near the blade.

I ripped my arm from her grasp, yanked the sword from the concrete, and shoved it through her bony chest. She dropped like a sack of rocks, and I dove into the car. "Let's go, let's go, let's go, let's go."

"Are you okay?" Monk asked. "You just *killed* her."

As if I hadn't noticed. "Yeah." I put the car in reverse and burned rubber back toward the street. "It happens. Tell me if they start chasing." There was an even chance that we'd be obliterated by oncoming traffic the second we popped out of the alley into the street, but given what was on the other end of the car, I thought it was a worthy risk.

At the mouth of the alley, I craned my neck as far back as I could then swung the wheel. The car swerved a little wide as its tires squealed, but we didn't die, so I called it a victory as I punched it forward. "Yes!"

Monk let out his breath. "Holy shit. What are we gonna do? Where are we gonna go?"

"Working on it." I pulled my phone from my pocket and tossed it into his lap. "Go into my email. Send a message to my contact named SplitScreen. Ask if she knows some-where safe we can stay for now."

Monk looked like he wanted to say something, but he wisely kept his mouth shut as he typed. A minute later, the app dinged. He looked at it. "She wants to know if you're okay, what happened, and what you found out, in that order." He paused. "And if you're alone."

"Well, I'm not, so you better announce yourself." I wasn't real happy about introducing Namiko and Silas Monk directly, given her history in Silicon Valley, but at this point, it couldn't be helped. I just hoped she would see it that way too. My email alert sounded a few more times. "What's she saying?"

"I think she's mad," said Monk. He sounded uncharac-teristically cowed. "Look, I recognize her handle. I've seen her stuff. I'm trying to tell her I don't necessarily disagree with everything she's said, or all the information she's uncovered, but she isn't—" He looked at the screen again. "She says to bring me to her house so she can look me in the face."

I held in a smirk. "Address? You might need to help me find it. I don't know the area."

"I'll tell it to you if you swear this girl isn't going to kill me when we get there."

"You'd rather deal with the harpies, huh? Trust me, Namiko is like two feet shorter than Eve. You can handle it."

Grudgingly, the richest tech mogul in Silicon Valley assumed the role of GPS, guiding me to my friend the computer espionage agent's house.

Life had not stopped being weird as hell.

Namiko lived in a wealthy, sprawling neighborhood where most of the giant houses had gates. Hers was gothic wrought-iron, topped with four-inch spikes that Monk eyed nervously.

"She is not going to impale you, okay? She's way too invested in this to ruin it now." I pulled up to the intercom box. A camera swiveled to face the car. "Hey, it's Vic. And… this guy." I jabbed my thumb in Monk's direction. "Sorry I had to bring him. It's a long story. Turns out his girlfriend was a harpy."

Namiko snorted.

"Hey! Am I the only one who thinks it would be cool if we didn't broadcast that information?" Monk asked.

"Pretty much," I said. The gate clicked and began to swing open. "Don't feel too bad. She might consider you humiliated enough not to torment you further."

"Great." He sulked all the way up the driveway and then all the way to her front door. Two more cameras examined us as we waited for her to let us in. A slot in the door, positioned precisely at Namiko-height, opened and closed in a flash, followed by the door itself.

She locked it three different ways behind us, repositioned the cameras, and primed a keypad. Then she led us down the front hall into a lofty, well-decorated living room. Noticing me staring at a wall of ornamental masks, she said, "This is my dad's old house, from when he was still working in the States. Those oni masks are his."

A laptop surrounded by three monitors was set up on the table in front of a leather couch. She posted herself in front of it and cast a disdainful glance at Monk. "Okay. So tell me how the hell this happened."

20

"Wow." Namiko pushed her laptop away so that she could fully absorb the craziness I'd just related to her. "All that shit you were talking before, about the Forgotten—vampires and gods and monsters—it's real? I...I'm not sure what to think about this."

"I know you don't care, but I can vouch for her," Monk said. "I was there too. Obviously."

She ignored him, getting back on her computer. "First things first, we should probably try to figure out who the guy in the trench coat is. He might be a problem if he's going to keep turning up everywhere."

"I know who he is." Monk's voice was weak. "Eve, she told me that I wouldn't be safe without her protection. She said that all manner of creatures would come for me."

"So what kind of creature is he?" Namiko asked.

"A demon," he said. "And he'll come for me again, I know it."

Namiko stared at him with an open mouth, then turned to me. "Is that possible?"

More than possible. Marcus's voice was tinged with worry. *And more than that, I know which demon he is. A particularly foul creature by the name of Abraxzael.*

"Abraxzael?" I said his name out loud before I had a chance to stop myself. Now it was their turn to look at me.

"Do *you* know him?" Namiko asked, somewhat suspiciously.

"What? No." I touched the links of the golden medallion chain. "This is going to be hard to explain, but as long as we're in this for the long haul, it might save us all some unnecessary confusion if I just told you." I held up the medallion for them to see. "The short version is that I had a friend at the beginning of this mess, he died, and he left me this. If I wear it, I can hear him."

"Can he read your mind?" Namiko wanted to know.

"I… don't know," I admitted. "I hope not."

I probably could if I wanted to, but I do not want to. I wish to continue respecting the established boundaries of our relationship.

"He says no. And he also says that he knows who the guy with the hammer is." We all waited expectantly.

That being is Brax, otherwise known as Abraxzael. He belongs to a subset of Forgotten called The Marked. They are akin to what you would call demons.

I sighed. "The dude goes by Brax. And Brax *is* a demon."

The blood drained from Monk's face. "We're all going to die."

"Just shut up nerd," Namiko shouted. Monk flinched when she spoke.

The term is merely the closest approximation I thought to make. I admit that I do not know as much about the Marked as others. During my tenure in Carcerum, I never bore witness to one. My predecessor, however, had multiple encounters with Abraxzael over the years, and your hammer wielding assailant fits the description.

"Well, what's his deal?" I moved over and sat down next to Namiko, motioning for Monk to join. "I won't lie; this is gonna be pretty weird. I can tell you what he says, but you're just going to have to trust me on it. Can you do that?"

Namiko didn't look happy, but she relented. I glanced at Monk. "If we all wear it together, would we be able to hear him?" he asked.

"I don't—" The question put me way more on the spot than I expected.

Namiko saved me. "There's no way I'm getting that close to you." She never looked up from her screen.

I cleared my throat as Monk retreated a few inches across the couch. "Sorry, Marcus. Please continue."

The history of the Marked is thus: They were the gods' first attempt at creating an enslaved race, but they proved too willful to subdue. After several failed rebellions, the largest of which resulted in many human casualties as well, the Marked were formally banished to their own realm.

Namiko and Monk stared at the medallion while I related Marcus' message. Namiko shot me a look. "Do you know how this works?"

"Ghost magic, as far as I can tell. He told me it holds the spirits of his ancestors. Anyway, why would Brax have a vendetta against Monk if he helped him build the drill?"

It is not the vendetta that worries me. It's what will happen if he gets ahold of the drill.

I grumbled. "That makes more sense to me than I want it to. It seems our sex goddess isn't the only one who wants your weapon."

"What can we do?" Monk was draining confidence by the second as the weight of his actions bore down on him.

"We have to make sure no one else gets it," I interjected. "Doesn't matter who or what stands in our way. You made it, it exists, and some really bad shits are trying to get their hands on it. But we can use this to our advantage. If this thing really is powerful enough to use in a fight against the gods, we need to secure it for our side. If the gods have a plan and that plan is coming to fruition, I want to have access to everything that will help us." Specifically, I wanted access to anything that would help *me*, but I kept that to myself, giving Monk a look. "It's not in your hotel room, is it? Please tell me it's not in there." Please tell me it's not already gone.

"Of course, it's not in there," he said, insulted. "The only one that exists right now is in my lab. I had it transported back there after the presentation at the Tech Institute."

"That settles it. We need to go back and get it."

"That's not going to be easy."

"Do you have a better idea?" Namiko cut in. I could have hugged her.

"Something that doesn't involve tons of law enforcement," Monk retorted. "They'll be all over us by the time we get there."

She frowned. "Right, because I'm sure the demon guy from hell cares about how many cops are guarding the thing he wants to steal. I would bet money that after you met him on the street, he decided you were too much trouble and he could take care of you after he recovered the tech. He's probably on his way out to your facility right now."

Monk wanted to disagree with her, vehemently, but he couldn't. He opened his mouth, inhaled, and closed it again. A cloud rolled in over his features. "He's going to get everything," he said quietly.

Namiko didn't answer, but she didn't twist the knife either. The tension in the room thickened.

"I know it doesn't look great right now," I said. "From any angle. But don't give up yet. I know a guy who may be able to help us with the cops."

"You know a guy who can stop an entire investigation?" Monk brightened. "Because if so, I can make you very, very rich."

"Gross," Namiko scoffed. "I'll be over here figuring out the best way to break into your place."

"Will you show me when you're done so I can better optimize security?" Monk asked.

She glared at him over the top of the screen. "No."

I SHUT the door to the next room behind me before breaking out my cell phone. Content to shun Monk with miles of icy silence, Namiko was happily at work devising a plan to break and enter, should that become necessary. For someone with the face and stature of a mid-teen at the oldest, she had the razor-sharp cunning of a seasoned criminal. And apparently, their joy of committing crimes.

"What a motley crew we are, huh, Marcus?"

I am concerned for your safety, Victoria. These are much larger risks than we ever had to take together, and you have only just made the acquaintance of both your partners.

"It could be better, and yeah, maybe I wish it was. But we don't have any other option, dude. We'd be doing the same shit if you were here, except I guess you'd at least have armor." I smiled. "Remember all that bullshit you said about being wrong about me? Just assume you're still wrong about me, and I'll come out of this kicking all kinds of ass."

Very well. I only wish that I was better able to assist in such a critical mission.

I stared at the phone in my hand. "You can join me in hoping Deacon doesn't bite my head off when I call him in three seconds." I grimaced. "It pains me to admit, but I need his help. I don't know jack about smooth-talking my way out of trouble. Usually, I just cause as much damage as I can."

Are you confident he will not simply inform his colleagues of your imminent arrival?

"If he does that, I'm going to be *pissed as shit*." I wanted to seem like I was joking, but inside, I had an identical fear. Yes, I liked Deacon, and under different circumstances, I would have tried harder to keep him coming around. But I was also keenly aware of our positions on either side of a certain line.

He didn't owe anything to me—in fact, I sort of owed him. He could have brought me in on suspicion of any number of things at the jail. He could've made sure I didn't get out before I hit middle age.

It felt pretty bad to be putting him on the ropes again. And yet, I did it anyway.

The world was at stake.

21

"DEACON ST. CLARE."

I'd sort of been hoping he would sound different this time. Uglier, maybe. No dice, he still sounded as smooth as they come. "Hey, it's Vic."

"Vic? Hold up." Footsteps sounded on his end of the line, followed by a door closing. Then he said, "What the hell are you doing out there?"

"Out there?" I shot back.

"Yeah. I saw the shots from the cameras in San Fran. The images are blurry enough that my people won't get a solid ID on you, but it won't fool me." He paused. "Why am I seeing you all over security cameras in some swanky hotel parking garage? Why are you stealing Aston Martins? This is not why I let you go."

"Whoa there, cowboy. I would just like to state for the record that the car I allegedly stole belongs to Silas Monk, and he is the one driving it in that video—even if they could see me. Okay? So it's not stolen. And also, you did not *let* me go, Deacon. You don't get to dictate my life because you don't own me."

He took a deep breath. "I'm sorry. That was out of line. But it doesn't make this shit you're pulling legal, Vic. Think about the position you're putting me in now that you, a wanted individual, has contacted me. Now I either have to lie for you or turn you in. I don't want to do either one of those."

I chewed my lip. "I'm sorry, too, because everything you just said is right, and I totally thought about it and called you anyway. I know this is really unfair of me, and I know I'm putting a lot on the line without your permission. I just... need help."

"And what, I'm the only one you can go to?" He didn't sound like he was buying it, which made me nervous. If he bailed, we'd have to wing it, and I wasn't real confident in Monk's or my ability to do that successfully.

"I mean, Jules is a public defender, but... she's a public defender, man. She's the public defender type. If I told her I needed advice on how to screw the law, she'd have an aneurysm on the spot."

"I'm not gonna give you advice on how to screw the law, either, whatever the hell that means." I could tell he was pacing by the cadence of his voice. "Look—what are you dealing with here? If you're trying to avoid charges or evade arrest, I really can't help you on the grounds that it would make me a criminal, too."

"What if I couched it in purely hypothetical terms that can't be proven to be rooted in reality?" I asked. "Then you'd be, like, a crime consultant. You'd be clarifying details in a theoretical case that is not at all real under any circumstances. Right?"

"Vic?"

I dared to put the smile back on. "What?"

"You're a real pain in the ass." He sank audibly into a chair. "Okay, okay. Hit me."

"Are you sure?"

"Dammit, woman, you spend five minutes sellin' me on hypotheticals and shit, and now that I've finally agreed, you ask me if I'm sure? You're trying me, Vic. You're really tryin' me." But there was the sound of a smile, if a little strained, under the veneer of frustration.

I laughed. "I'm sorry. Let me make it up to you when I get back."

"Yeah, yeah. Lay this thing on me before someone comes busting in here and sends us both to jail. Not too many details, okay? I still need my plausible deniability."

"All right. Say there's something really important we need, but we have to get through a police or FBI barricade. What would we say to get access?"

"That depends. Is it a murder scene?"

"No. I don't think so."

Deacon paused. "No, I'm not even gonna ask. Robbery?"

"Maybe."

"Vic, if it's a robbery you committed, I'm going to have to strongly recommend you do not return to the scene."

I laughed again. "Screw you, St. Clare. I have not committed any robberies as of late." Too late, I realized I'd forgotten about the grey hatchback, which was now sitting in Namiko's driveway. Although technically, that was grand theft auto. "No, it might be a robbery depending on whether or not we're too late."

He groaned at that. "It's like, I want to know, but I also don't want you to tell me, like ever. You're lucky I'm not stationed out there." For the third or fourth time, he sighed. "All I can tell you is this. You don't really have any say in whether or not they let you by, unless you're their superior. If you've got someone with you who owns the place or lives there, that could help your case a bit, but not always."

"That's not much, Deacon. How is that supposed to help me?"

"Look, I can't say more without feeling like I'm aiding and abetting a crime. It all depends on the individual circumstances, including the specific agents you're talking to. Some of them are dicks."

"I'm surprised you'd admit that, given your current profession."

He laughed. "How do you think I know?

"Thanks, Deacon. I owe you one, or five. I guess." The phone went silent for a second, and I checked the screen to see if we were still connected. "Deacon?"

"Yeah. Still here." Silence again, and then he spoke in a hush. "Okay. There's one more thing I shouldn't tell you. This could get me into deep shit."

"It's the only shit I know," I answered with a grin.

Deacon laughed from the other side of the country. "Listen, you need to keep this between us, but it's about Monk. He's on a list."

"Shit. What? Like *al qaeda*?"

"No. Not yet. The bureau keeps a list of guys like him,

tech guys. There's a slew of them that make it onto the list, but some of them get upgraded. A few weeks ago, Silas Monk got an upgrade."

"Upgrade?"

"Yeah. Just being on the list means he's working on something that could be of interest to national security. Getting an upgrade means either he's made suspicious contacts or something that would raise an analyst's eyebrows and make his asshole pucker. I can't tell what it is by just looking but…"

After a beat, I asked, "But what?"

"But… Don't trust him, OK?"

I glanced up at the doorway, not knowing where Monk, or Namiko for that matter, was. Playing it safe, I answered, "Yeah. Sure. You got it."

"Do something else for me, and be careful. Whatever it is you're up to. I know you're a little crazy, but I want to know you're looking out for yourself."

I chuckled. "I'm the only one I look out for. See you later. And Deacon...thanks."

I hung up on him to save us both the agonizing awkwardness of trying to end that call in any other way. Taking a moment to collect myself and force the redness from my cheeks through sheer power of will, I slipped my phone into my bag and ran my fingers through my hair. "I am going to go back out there, we're gonna nail down a plan, and then we're going to execute. Flawlessly. Like always."

That last part might not be entirely true, but a little optimism couldn't hurt.

Namiko looked up from her screen as I crossed the threshold. "Hi. What did your friend say?"

"Hang on." I panned my gaze left, then right. "Where the hell is Monk? He wasn't stupid enough to ditch now, was he?"

Namiko's eyes widened. "I didn't even notice he wasn't here anymore. Maybe I was ignoring him too hard." She did a full spin on the couch and found nothing new. "It's a big house. He could be lost."

"Okay, but why is he sneaking around in the first place? He was kind of growing on me, but this sets him way back."

"That's a shame. You were growing on me, too." Both of us jumped and whirled to glare at the doorway where Silas Monk was now standing. He grinned at us. "A guy can't go to the bathroom once in a while?"

"You never asked me where it was," Namiko said accusingly.

"It's a bathroom. I figured it couldn't be that hard to find. Spoiler alert: it wasn't."

Namiko looked extremely dissatisfied by this explanation, and I couldn't blame her. It didn't sit right with me, either, but now I knew we needed him for the next step. "Don't do shit like that," I told him, meeting as close to the middle as I could. "If you have to go somewhere, tell us. We thought you got kidnapped again."

"Sorry. You're right. I just didn't want to disturb her since I think she's annoyed just knowing I exist."

Namiko muttered, "You're not wrong."

I rolled my eyes. "I have a plan, you guys, so listen up." To their credit, they both actually looked at me. "My—"

Namiko's computer beeped. She glanced at the screen, and her face dropped. "Oh, shit."

"What's wrong?" Her expression told me exactly what was wrong.

"The cops are here."

Reflexively, I turned toward her front door, even though I couldn't see anything from the living room. "How many are there?"

A knock rang out down the front hall.

"Police!" someone called. "Open up!"

Namiko whispered, "There are a lot." She turned the laptop toward me to show the policemen filling both camera screens. My mind raced, trying to come up with one more, last ditch, miraculous solution.

There was none. The jig was up. Silas Monk seemed to know it, too. He ran his hand over his face, and his whole body deflated. He glanced at me.

"I can't fight cops," I said. "No, wait. I *won't* fight cops."

"No, yeah." He nodded. "I understand. I'm not a fighter anyway." Truer words had never been spoken, but I let it slide.

"Let's just get this over with," I said and let Namiko lead us to the door. She popped the locks and cracked it open.

"All the way," said the officer in front. "We're not here to hurt anybody." Reluctantly, Namiko stepped back. As soon as he saw me and Monk, the cop got on his radio. "We got 'em. They'll be in for questioning in about twenty minutes."

Monk went first to be led down into the driveway. They didn't shackle him, and he looked back before he got in the squad car, meeting my eyes for a split second. He was so hang-dog that I was suddenly awash in both pity and guilt, and that made the concept of questioning and jail seem like something I might just deserve this time.

"Don't look so worried, ma'am. We just want to find out what you know." My cop was handsome: dirty blond, rugged jawline, blue eyes. He had the kind of smile that made him a shoo-in for violent crime units; victims' families would cling to him in the midst of their own personal storms.

I didn't trust him. He reminded me of things I had tried and failed over and over to forget.

"Let's go," I said quietly.

"Vic—" Namiko's fingers brushed the back of my arm. She'd never looked smaller than she did right then, still half inside the doorway and completely helpless. The house looked like it was swallowing her.

I smiled, hoping it came out more convincing than it felt. "I'll be fine, Namiko. Everything will be fine."

Then I faced forward again and saw someone weaving through the crush of squad cars jammed into the driveway. Her bloodred hair gleamed.

When I noticed her, she was looking at Namiko. Then her gaze shifted directly to me. I hardened my face, determined to communicate the explicit disgust with which I associated her whole kind. Instead of responding with anger of her own, she smiled.

That was a thousand times worse.

22

"See? That wasn't so bad." The cop had a deliberately gentle hand on my elbow as he guided me toward his cruiser. "You don't have to be cuffed. We're just going to talk."

"That's fine." Thirty seconds ago, it *had* been fine. Now that I knew who was behind this whole situation, it was mostly just enraging. Still not enough to make me want to hurt cops, but I could definitely fight some.

As for the boss bitch, she was going down.

I stood with my hand on the car door, monitoring the red-headed harpy's progress. Every step seemed to make her grow, and by the time she reached speaking distance, she towered over everyone around her. I had seen it before in the warehouse, but face to face, the effect was daunting.

I hated having to look so far up to make eye contact with her.

And I hated the pure objectiveness of her beauty. There wasn't a single flaw on her body, not even an out of place hair. The constant smile on her lips widened as she finished closing the remaining distance, waving the rugged officer away. He didn't resist or even ask her any questions. He just left.

"Must be nice to have an inexhaustible source of mindless slaves," I remarked.

"I like to think it's nice for them, too. You'll know what it's like soon enough." A slight frown creased her forehead. "Unless I decide to just finish you off. You've proven to be a little too feisty."

"Yeah." I rubbed the toe of my shoe in the dirt. "Turns out I don't like it when Earth gets overrun by a bunch of power hungry monsters."

She giggled, flashing me a glint of deceptively sharp teeth behind her rosy lips. Like when I spoke with Eve, a warm sensation crept over my skin. Except this time, instead of bringing me a calming peace, all I could feel was rage. The buzzing sound when she spoke was like a gnat flitting near my ear, waiting to be squashed.

"Aren't you precious?" she continued. "Power hungry monsters took this world the moment the gods left— they're called humans." A malicious light crept into her eyes, behind which I saw nothing except vanity and ruthless pride. "Give Earth over to my goddess, and she will make it into an oasis."

"Somehow, I doubt that very, very much." I gestured to the scene around us, the cops, the cars, and the flashing lights. "How about this? You call off your dogs, and we settle this one on one."

"A tempting offer," she said thoughtfully. "But no. Why would I rid myself of such an advantage just to guarantee a lesser being a fair fight? That is not a logical course of action. However..." She grinned cruelly. "If a fight is what you want, then that's what you will get."

As she finished speaking, I realized two things. One: her minions were closing in on me. Two: it was suddenly very dark. Glancing up, I saw that the latter was because she had spread her wings, blocking out the sun with their expanse.

"Oh, shit." The beat of those wings sent the driveway gravel spinning. She looped her way into the sky, until all I could see was a vague shape. I wrenched my gaze back to Earth. She'd come down eventually. And I'd deal with her when she got here.

A quick assessment of the situation told me things were not good. The harpy was the only one I had any sort of beef with. She was just using the cops as a bunch of human shields.

But as I looked at them now, I realized they weren't humans at all. They were vampires.

Anger flooded my veins as they closed in and I lashed out with my bare fists. I was tired of taking it easy on these bastards. I barely felt it when my fists connected with jaws and stomachs and noses, but I heard the shrieks of pain and hunger as my enemies fell. The power in my arms was dangerously intoxicating.

Somewhere in the back of my mind, I heard a voice calling out to me. But I couldn't focus on it. There was only the rage and the fight. The howls of the swarming vamps buzzed in my ears as I tore through them, breaking limbs and dropping bodies to the ground. They started to flee before me, terrified by the force I had become.

I gave chase, then stopped as a large figure stepped in front of me.

It was Rocco Durant.

He snarled at me with his wide, toothy grin, like he had on the day I chased him down the docs.

"You," I shouted. "You're dead."

He opened his mouth to speak, but only laughed instead. It filled me with a fire I had never known before. Without thinking, the sword was in my hands. I felt like I could cut a mountain in half, but I didn't need to go that far. All I needed was to end this miserable life.

I raised the blade high, and Rocco transformed into the monster he had become on the day I last saw him. The day I killed him.

The day Marcus died.

Marcus.

Something wasn't right, and my blade wavered. Rocco beat his chest but he stayed rooted to the ground. A faint voice called out to me and I reached for it.

Vic...Vic...you are under her spell.

"Marcus...I..." I blinked and suddenly the world changed. Gone was the buzzing, the heat, the anger. And the figure standing in front of me wasn't my parents' killer, but a terrified looking Namiko.

I dropped to my knees, the blade extinguished by my side.

"Are you, OK?" Namiko asked. She stared at me wide eyed like her whole world had been turned upside down.

"I'm so sorry, Namiko," I choked out. "It was the harpy, I was under her spell."

"I know," she said. "I saw her, the woman from the warehouse, talking to you. Then she turned into this hideous creature and you went nuts."

I lifted my head sharply. "The vamps."

Spinning around, I saw a dozen police officers rolling around in the dirt. They weren't vampires at all, just men and women trying to do their job.

"Shit. Go to them," I said. "Make sure they're OK."

Namiko nodded. "What are you going to do?"

"I'm going to go clip that bitch."

I grabbed my sword and marched past the cars and fallen officers. I could see the harpy waiting for me, floating near the end of the driveway.

"You're with me, aren't you, Marcus?"

Always.

"I don't know if I'll be able to keep her out of my head. I can't trust myself."

Then trust in me. Follow my voice, and I will guide you.

I nodded. Time to end this charade.

"My, my." The harpy's shadow fell over me as I walked near. "It looks like our little rat is smarter than we imagined." She flapped her wings above, eyeing me with a predator's vision. The wind blew my hair back. "Let's fix that, shall we?"

The creature dropped like a stone from the sky, aiming for me with deadly purpose. Her long claws snaked out toward my throat.

The wide end of Namiko's driveway was empty, her heavy gate closed. This was what I had wanted from the beginning. And I was prepared to follow through.

I dodged, but she was too fast. The feel of her nail edge scraping my skin set me back into battle mode, no holds barred. The sword seemed to jump into my hand as if it had been waiting for me to snap out of it. Nothing had ever felt as good as that first hard swing. I missed, but it didn't matter. The only thing of any importance was that I was fighting the way I wanted to fight so that I could win the way I wanted to win.

This harpy was either more agile than the others I had fought before, or she was just more filled with bullshit. She was constantly half a step ahead of me, dancing mockingly just out of my reach. All of my swings, no matter how sure I was that they'd land, left little more than scratches. She was doing it on purpose; I felt it. Pushing me to the brink of my tolerance. Trying to break through the armor I thought I'd built up.

Concentrate, Victoria. Call on the fire in your soul to sustain you. Your heart is true. She cannot corrupt it.

"No, it's not. There's a lot of shit wrong with my heart, Marcus, and you know it. I'm just too damn stubborn to let it go this way."

All this hit-and-miss wasn't helping. I was wasting my energy pool, which, although extended considerably, remained finite. I could feel the strain of a battle that had gone on far too long wearing on me in more ways than one.

And then suddenly there were three of her.

I stopped mid-swing and blinked. Three perfect copies

of this redheaded crone flew before me. They swooped in for an attack.

I slashed outward at the first, but my blade passed through it as if it were made of smoke. The second veered toward my right, and while I was distracted by it something plowed into me. A huge chunk of skin was ripped from my side.

All three figures rushed skyward—all I could hear was their laughter.

"Marcus…"

It's another one of her tricks, but you can beat this. Steel your nerves. Wait for my word.

The three harpies turned around for another attack, screeching the whole way. The one in front came at me with raised claws. They were aiming for my eyes, ready to gouge at my face.

Steady.

I didn't even blink as the mirage passed through me.

The second buzzed overhead, trying to get me to take the bait, but I held my ground and waited for number three.

Now!

The moment Marcus spoke I sprang into action. Like I was chopping a log, the *Gladius Solis* swung overhead. Blood and feathers rained down around me and I heard a wail like a bat caught in a cage.

I turned around to see the harpy flopping in the dirt, one wing completely severed from her body.

"How dare you." Her voice was gnarled, rasping against my eardrums. She bent like a tree in a tornado. "You have *defiled* me!"

"And I'm just getting started." I rotated the blade smoothly with my wrist, rebalancing its weight. "You can keep trying if you want, but we both know the game is over. The ending is up to you now."

She stared at me, her eyes bugged and wild. The thin lips pulled back from jagged teeth, parting in a brutal scream.

She launched herself toward me.

"The hard way it is, then," I said as I raised my sword.

"Vic?"

Hearing the sound of my name was like breaking the still surface of a lake after a deep, cold dive. I turned around, refreshed and seeing the world with new—or at least changed—eyes. Namiko's face took a moment to register in my mind. I figured she'd be terrified or revulsed by me, but the expression she wore was one of concern. Compassion. And a hint of triumph.

"You did it," she said as she reached a hand down to help me to my feet.

"With some help," I smiled. "How are the girls and boys in blue?"

She shrugged. "Pretty banged up, but they'll live. None of them seem to know what's going on though. It's like they're waking up from a coma. How hard did you hit them?"

"Pretty hard, but I'd wager their confusion is our redheaded friend's doing."

She nodded as we walked toward them. "So what can I do to help. What's next?"

"Find Monk," I said. "Quick. If we get out of here before they recognize us, they'll leave eventually. You stay here and make sure that happens. There aren't any outstanding warrants in your name, are there?"

Namiko raised her chin proudly. "I always cover my tracks."

"Good." My roving eye spotted Monk standing awkwardly against the side of a police car, arms folded. "Ugh. Does he think he looks like he belongs there?" Moving as fast as I dared to risk, I beelined to him. "Get over here. We're leaving."

"Fine by me." He frowned. "What the hell was all that?"

"Shut up and take me to your lab," I said.

23

Monk was driving again, much more safely than last time. We had snagged a car on our way out of Namiko's neighborhood, and now I sat in the passenger seat in silence, my last fight swirling in my head. He asked no questions, which was good. Somehow, I didn't think he'd understand what had really happened. Hell, I didn't know what it looked like outside of my own perspective. Just good old Vic, taking down law enforcement.

How badly had she gotten to me? There was no way to know. I feared it would bother me for the rest of my life.

Onto the next stage of your quest, Victoria. There will be time for reflection later. Remember what Deacon told you.

I rubbed my hands over my face. Deacon was the last thing I wanted on my mind right now. I could just hear him, the way he'd sounded on the phone, grappling with a conflict I thought I knew all too well.

He wanted to fix me. But fixing meant helping. And helping me meant trouble for him.

That was why this damn drill was so important. The LIGHT was the thing that could help me push back against the gods like I meant it. I was sorely in need of some kick-ass instruments of deity destruction.

"Do you think it's still there?" I asked Monk. The answer was something I'm not sure either of us wanted to think about, let alone vocalize, but now that the edge had fallen off my melancholy, I found the silence suffocating. At least if we were breaking and entering, I'd have something to take my mind off what a broken mess I still was.

"It better be, or I'm really going to need to overhaul my security systems." He talked like he was joking, but his eyes were steely. "I think they should let me in since I own the place, but I guess you never know. How's your sweet-talking skill?"

I bit my lip. "We're about to find out."

———

MONK INDUSTRIES WAS HOUSED in a starkly white building with clean, modern lines that gleamed in the lengthening sunlight. Almost immediately, I picked out a set of flashing red and blue lights. "Yep, here we go."

"Lot's gonna be full of them, I bet," Monk muttered. His eyes started to shift nervously, fingers tapping against the wheel. "Let's hope they don't decide to run this plate."

"Wouldn't that be something." We turned the last bend before the approach to the front of the massive building, and even in the current situation, I was struck momentarily dumb by the scale of Monk's pioneer operation. "Nice digs." I said, when I found my voice.

"Thanks. That view never gets old." There were more lights clustered in a little knot near the walkway up to the doors but not nearly as many as I'd dreaded.

"Why's it so quiet here?" I asked. "I'm not really complaining, but it makes me nervous."

Monk grimaced. "Me too. Feels like an ambush."

I was pretty sure he said that just to seem cool, but distressingly, he wasn't wrong. My heartbeat picked up as we pulled into a spot not too close to the cruisers. They were silent—lights only.

Was it an omen?

Huffing at myself, I rolled my eyes. The last thing I needed right now was to be soaking up crazy superstitions. Gods I could deal with, so far. I shut the car door and started walking toward the curb without checking to see if Monk was behind me.

"Hey, are you gonna be all right?" he asked, jogging briefly to catch up with me. "You've been different since we left that house."

"I don't want to talk about it." He didn't seem convinced, so I added, "Really. It would be too hard to explain."

"I don't know. You've done a decent job with everything else."

"I appreciate the compliment, but you don't have to." I paused before reaching out to one of the frosted glass doors. "Is there anything in here I need to watch out for? Security droids? Lasers? Highly trained ninja operatives?"

"It's probably already disabled if they're in there some-where." Monk peered through the glass. "I can't see anything. Want me to go first?"

"No. I don't think you could protect me from a pack of kittens, Monk." I gritted my teeth and yanked open the door.

He followed, grumbling, "I could if they were declawed."

THE INTERIOR WAS vast and open… and empty of everything except ridiculously fancy cars. It looked like the inside of a recently abandoned building, so quiet and deep were the shadows. I caught myself breathing shallowly, as if that would help me hear the stillness better. It didn't sit right with me.

Even if the cops had already processed this floor, they should've been posted up on a perimeter, just in case. I'd seen enough search sites to know there was something seriously jacked up with this one.

"Be careful." My whisper carried much too far in all the wide-open space. "I don't know where they are."

"Upstairs, maybe. Or downstairs. There are a lot of levels in this place."

I pinched the bridge of my nose. The longer we spent in this place, the greater my anxiety built. "Where do *we* need to be?" Hopefully, he'd get the hint and not make me elaborate.

"All the way on the bottom. This way."

The elevator didn't play music as it sunk us down below the first floor. I kept my eyes fixed on the digital floor counter, trying to ignore all the drastic possibilities piling up in my mind. Maybe there was another harpy in charge of the police force that came here, and they were long gone with the drill. Maybe there was no drill at all, and it was all a weird, elaborate con. Maybe Monk and Brax were actually the same person somehow, and he was waiting for the most dramatic moment to unveil himself.

The elevator sang out a pleasant tone. Its doors slid open a hundred feet from the biggest vault door I'd ever seen.

"*Voila*," Monk sang. Seeing his vault seemed to wipe the stress clean away. I wished I had that kind of instant-off switch.

"Okay, it's gotta be in there," I said. "I'm not sure even my magic sword could cut through that."

Yes, it could. Fortunately, it is the only thing that could.

"I'd say you could give it a shot, but we're pressed for time." He put his palm up against a hidden panel, then pressed each fingertip and his thumb in specific locations on the face of the door. A massive bolt freed itself somewhere within. "Come on." He patted one of the prongs on the gigantic lock-wheel. "It takes two to crack this baby open. On a good day."

He wasn't exaggerating. We fought that thing for three whole minutes before it started to budge, a problem I was confident originated with his perfectly average upper body. He was almost hanging on it before the wheel decided to turn. Then he dropped off and put his hand back on the hidden plate. "Stand back."

The door slid out on an arc of embedded tracks, passing a wall of lasers over both of us. I put my hand in my bag, running my thumb over the now-familiar contours of the hilt. It gave me comfort but not enough. The anxiety was crushing.

Not that the vault would be full of cops or that I'd find all the disappeared New York vamps waiting for me inside. I was just terrified that the LIGHT would be gone. And if it was, I'd be well and truly fucked, along with the rest of humanity.

Yeah, maybe the pressure was getting to me a little. I could have ripped Monk's head off for coughing. The door crept along its tracks so slowly I wanted to blow it to pieces. "Can't you make it go faster?"

"No. It's so heavy it's a safety risk if it goes too quickly. There'd be no way to save someone who got caught."

I bounced from foot to foot just to relieve the jitters threatening to overtake my composure. Call me insane, but I hadn't anticipated so much waiting.

Little did I know, things were about to pick up real quick.

"Hey!" The voice cracked out down the short hall like a gunshot. Silas Monk flinched and moved to cover his head. I spun around, sword brandished.

I wonder if he realizes how lucky he is that you are here, Marcus mused.

"I guarantee he doesn't." I spoke through clenched teeth, staring a black uniform in the eye. He was pointing a gun directly at my face.

"Hands up. Drop the weapon!"

Raising my free hand, I kept a firm grip on the hilt. His eyes flicked back and forth so quickly I thought he might pass out. "Look to my right," I suggested. "See who's with me. And then please put down your gun."

The guy flicked his broad, square head toward Monk, squinted, and did a double take. "Wait. Sir?"

Monk brought his arms cautiously down. "Uh…" He looked at the name patch. "Yeah. Hey, Joe. You working late tonight?"

"Shit, it's *really* you." His suspicion toward me only lessened marginally. "Do you know her?"

"Oh, yeah. Yeah. She's cool." Monk kept glancing toward the gun, licking his lips. Sweat was starting to bead on his temples. He wiped his face. "So, everything is fine, right? Where is everyone?"

Joe blinked. "Sir…" He looked between us, rapid fire. It was clear I was missing some subtext, and I wasn't sure I wanted to know what it was. "Yes," he said at last. "Everything is fine." He unhooked a walkie talkie from his belt. "I'll tell the others to stand down."

"Much appreciated," Monk said. "I'd rather not be murdered at work."

I eyed the back of Joe's head as he hurried back toward the elevator, trying to decide if I should take him down or not. My instincts were screaming at me that the whole place stank of something fishy.

Leave him, Marcus said. *But do not trust him.*

Forcing myself to be satisfied with Marcus's assessment, I turned back to follow Monk into the now-open vault.

Or him.

Monk shot a look over his shoulder from where he stood in the center of the vault's opening. "Good news," he said. "The LIGHT is right in front of me."

24

I started forward, the cumulation of all my nervous excitement bursting in my chest. The whole ordeal in San Francisco thus far started to fade away in the brightness of this stroke of luck. I wouldn't allow myself to hope that it was all worth it now, but it was a start.

Then Monk stepped aside, and the house of cards on which I'd built my hope came crashing down again.

That's when I saw her.

If nothing else, at least he hadn't exaggerated her height. She was even taller than the redhead I'd killed at Namiko's house—and infinitely more striking. Dark hair cascaded down her back in a torrent, framing a face adorned with ruby-red lips and soft, hypnotizing eyes. The kind of face I could have stared at forever. The white dress flowed around her like it was liquid, pooling at her feet.

I stopped dead in my tracks, semi-aware that my jaw was in the process of unhinging itself. The logical part of my brain told me she had to be another hallucination. There was no way she could be real.

She put her hand on Monk's shoulder, its weight creasing the fabric of his shirt. He looked up at her and slipped from her grasp, moving deeper into the vault. Her eyes settled on me then and turned me into a straight-up window. The red lips curved upward.

"So," she said. "We meet at last, slayer of beauty. Do you know who I am?"

Just like Delano's misty stare had left me powerless the first time I saw him, her voice stole the air from my lungs. All I could do was nod wordlessly, standing dumbstruck in front of the elevator. No part of my body worked until she beckoned me forward, giving me permission to move.

"Don't be shy," she said. "I won't bite...unless you want me to."

Shy or not, I had no choice. The woman was like a magnet, and she clearly wasn't taking no for an answer. I wanted to ask Marcus what the hell was going on, but I suspected that every thought I had was an open book for her. And I'd already gotten the poor dude killed; I didn't want to get him exorcised, too.

"Tsk, tsk." She backed up as the distance closed, drawing me along with her into the vault. "There is nothing you can hide from me." Her finger drew its way over the neckline of my shirt, brushing aside a loose strand of hair. "I know all about your beloved stowaway, but you don't have to worry. He can't help you now anyway." Suddenly seizing the medallion's chain in her fist, she tore it from my neck and tossed it away. "Let me free you from your burdens, Victoria. All of them."

I flinched, already feeling the flesh bruising at the back of my neck where the chain dug in. Her hand came back toward me to caress my face. The pad of her thumb ran over my lips. "Do you want your voice back, my newest love?" she murmured.

My skin crawled. Mythical powers of attraction or not, something about this woman's touch repulsed me despite my inability to resist it. It was clear she knew that—and enjoyed it immensely. I pressed my lips into a grim line and tried to pull away. One syllable dropped off my tongue. "No."

She arched her eyebrows. "No? Then you must want me to rip that pretty tongue of yours right out of your mouth." She laughed, teeth flashing. "I know your mind is troubled. You have been polluted by the influence of Kronin's lackey soldier. Forget him. He is nothing. And Kronin is gone." Her ample breasts hovered in front of my face as she leaned in toward me. "I am all you need."

Her hand snaked behind my head, fingers plunging into my hair, and she pulled me against her like a fly in her web.

All my senses filled with her scent, her touch, and the lusty beat of her heart inside her chest. She overwhelmed me, leaking into every facet of my being. Marcus had called it brainwashing, but this was a bigger experience than that. My will was being smothered out of existence.

The one word I'd managed to speak came back to me with the intensity of a lightning strike. I forced my mouth to open, even though she had me pinned against the razor-sharp definition of her clavicle.

"No," I mumbled again. More energy gathered behind it. "No. No!" I threw my head back. Her grip faltered. "No!"

She released me, her gaze colored by a mix of surprise and bitter offense. "Well, well. It's been a long time since I last encountered a will like this. You're lucky I enjoy a challenge." Again, her thumb touched my mouth, the nail digging not-so-gently into the flesh. "But I would very much appreciate it if you learned another word." Her grip tightened abruptly on my chin, the bones crushing the sides of my jaw. The bitch was elegant, but she held on like a vise. "Say my name."

I stayed silent. The goddess, if that was really what she was, applied more pressure. As a counterpoint, I clenched my teeth, making sure she felt the resistance. Her eyes turned cold and cruel. "I can play your silly little games for *eternity*, street harlot. You dare display such flagrant hubris before me? I will make you kneel." She dropped my chin and turned away to compose herself.

My tongue moved in my mouth, working to gain back its independence. When Eve had almost charmed me into giving away the *Gladius Solis*, it was because she made me see her side of things. She'd made me share her desires.

Lysiani wasn't doing that for me. There was too dark an edge of inhumanity beneath her perfect exterior, boiling just beneath the surface.

I'd seen far too much of that already, far too close to home. No matter how she tried, nothing could cover it up.

"Perhaps," she began, feigning an air of contrite boredom, "I should learn from you and exercise a rare hint of humility. Let me take a step back and explain my reasoning. I should not have expected you to rise to the level of a queen." She circled around me, approaching slyly from the back, a predator I could feel but not see. "Doubtless you have heard from my sisters how we aspire to change this wretched place for the better. From good and evil, we will create Eden.

"However, not all of our contemporaries share our vision of harmony for the future." She ran a hand through her gleaming hair, letting it cascade across her shoulders. "Gods are brutish beings, my love. A damn foul lot. Sometimes they must be corrected. And sometimes, that correction must come through force."

"Kronin," I whispered.

Lysiani's glance was full of knives. "Oh, child. Your delusions fill me with sadness. I only wish I had reached you before that sniveling armored servant. Kronin was a tyrant who only sought to secure power for himself. He saw no distinction between a queen's great vision and the heinous machinations of demons. None of us mattered to him, you see? He loved *humanity* above all else. And ultimately, it was his failure that sealed your fate. It takes a stronger love than he had to offer. A mother's love, that knows when to bless—and when to punish."

She paced a few feet away from me, gesticulating with her slender hands. "I have spent more time than is necessary or fair contemplating how Kronin came to be blessed with the *Gladius Solis*. For all the time during which he ruled from cursed Carcerum, the odds have been stacked against those of us who were considered lesser than the hero-king. Now, at last, we have a chance to make things right."

She stopped pacing, swooped in, and grasped my face in her talons, digging tracks in the skin of my cheeks. "You are chosen to bear witness to the final delivery of justice."

A familiar voice emerged from behind her. "Your Majesty, the LIGHT is ready."

"Ah, yes. Thank you, my beautiful gift from the cosmos." She touched Monk's cheek, and a crimson bloom erupted beneath her fingers. A goofy grin spread across his face. She was the world to him. There was nothing else. "Let us show our guest the future."

As soon as he regained command of his faculties, Monk strutted to the center of the room where the drill, now free of its protective glass case, sat embedded in a square pedestal. His smile widened as he reached out and thumbed a heavily wired button in the base. A low frequency permeated everything. The air seemed to vibrate around every solid object in the room.

"Let us go," I said. My voice was stronger now, more demanding. It caught Lysiani's attention right away

"You poor thing." She pressed her lush lips to my forehead, the tender, kind façade back in place. "I have been brutish to you, haven't I? I have stooped to the very level I condemn. For that hypocrisy, I must offer atonement. Be free."

Her hold lifted from me. I stumbled under my own weight but caught myself before my knees hit the floor. Lysiani stood over me, her face shadowed. Behind her, the drill's core was glowing. The room blazed in high contrasts, a sterile hell lit by destruction.

"It won't save you," I said. "The drill isn't enough to beat all the other gods. They will tear you down."

Lysiani gazed at me inscrutably. Her eyes were made dark from the harsh glow of the drill; bottomless hungry pits. "This is why I have not killed you," she said softly.

"This is why I have allowed you and the sword, which is not even yours, to hew ragged slices in the bodies of my tribe. This is why I met you here instead of simply absconding with this jewel of destruction." She licked her lips. "Because I want you for my own."

I backed away toward the curving wall of the vault. At first, Lysiani stayed where she was, but when I strayed too far from her reach and too close to the drill, she began to prowl after me. I could feel myself returning with greater and greater presence as the remnants of her touch released their hold on me. Monk could be enraptured by a harpy's gaze alone. Not me. Not anymore.

"I would die before I joined you," I said.

"Then you will. And what a senseless waste of potential it will be. You could become the greatest apprenti ever created, Victoria, the demigoddess who utilizes her omniscient power to infuse whole galaxies with gracious compassion. I offer you the solution to all strife, all violence, all war. But you would rather die."

I scoffed. "It doesn't work like that. Trust me, I've been carving a path of vengeance across New York City for half a decade, and you know what? My parents are still dead."

"Ah, but so is their killer, isn't he?" Lysiani eyed me keenly. "As I am sure you have long since deduced on your own, Lorcan's abominations came to the west coast. They were sent to infiltrate us, to filch what data they could on our weapon. Instead, they died. Well, at least the ones who were sent."

"So much for harmony, huh?"

"Of course not. A being which cannot exist in harmony with others may be justifiably eliminated. Lorcan's feckless minions conducted all their business by means of blood and violence, and in the end, we were forced to reciprocate." The goddess shrugged. "Unsurprising, if you ask me. The apprenti Delano is his only half-decent servant. Now that one *could* be something, if he would only step out of Lorcan's shadow. But I digress."

She lifted her chin. "The natural order always wins out in the end. Your parents are dead, but they can only die once. The vampires can kill again and again and again. How many lives like those of your parents have you saved with each vampire you destroyed? Surely, the number is countless."

I wanted to recoil, to keep putting distance between us, but she had struck on the one line of reasoning that had comforted me many nights. The notion of justice was one I had clung to for so long that it became my only truth.

Yes, there were casualties in this fight. Yes, some damage was collateral. But at the end of the day, I was saving more lives than I lost. And if that were extrapolated to the level of a goddess, maybe Lysiani was right. Maybe I was too small-time to end the cycle of violence enveloping my own mortal life, but risen beyond my limits, there was so much more at stake.

I didn't trust Lysiani. I doubted I would ever trust her. But if she became my equal and my ally, I could mitigate her mercurial passions, shield worlds of innocents from her wrath.

Wouldn't that just be fast-tracking me to the end of the mission I had been given? What better way to stop the war from happening than to become a key player in its development? Having been an exceptionally stubborn human, I could stand my ground no problem. Plus, I had the *Gladius Solis* on my side.

"You have nothing to lose," Lysiani was saying, "and so much to gain." She gestured toward the LIGHT drill, now a radiant eye of steadily building energy. "Is that not the most beautiful thing you've ever seen? If it were yours, you could wield it only as you wish. To protect the weak. To punish the cruel. To heal the myriad wounds on your planet's once-beautiful face." Lysiani stepped close. "Imagine it. I beseech you."

I almost did, but then my foot came down on an object that warmed the sole through the bottom of my boot. Jolted from a near fugue state, I glanced down and saw a golden aura battling with the bluish shine of the drill.

"Don't you dare," Lysiani hissed. She'd recognized the medallion, too, and her rage seethed to the surface. "We are so close, *Victoria*. So close. You would forsake all potential for nothing?"

In one swift motion, I bent down and snatched the length of chain from the floor. As soon as the gold touched my skin, Marcus erupted in my ear.

Fight, Victoria! Fight! Resist her!

My eyes met the harpy queen's one more time. "You wanted me to call you Lysiani."

FIGHT!

She scowled.

I said, "Don't fucking call me *Victoria*."

"I AM A GODDESS! I will call you whatever I please." Her expression hardened into a mask of wrath and vengeance. She jerked her hand away from me, baring her teeth with in a sneer. Backed by the bright, burning light of the drill, her beauty, still great, became terrible.

"I'm going to make this very clear to you," I said calmly. The storm in my mind and heart was gone, replaced by a serenity that would have been eerie if it wasn't so comfortable. "Call me Victoria again and I will carve you like a Christmas goose."

"Weakling whelp!" Lysiani raised the point of her chin. "I would love to see you try."

I summoned Kronin's blade so close to her face that its sudden blast of heat rippled the hair away from her skin. She gasped, flinched backward.

"What's wrong?" I asked. "Are you scared?"

Her eyes burned with undisguised hatred. "Let this be a lesson to you, ungrateful human swine. Everything I have was yours to take, yours to conquer. Now I have no choice but to follow through on the philosophy I foolishly believed you'd understand. All sources of imbalance must be eliminated."

Mimicking her stance and her previous challenge, I answered, "I would love to see you try."

She snarled. "As you wish." Bracing myself for a screeching charge, I was a little surprised to see her step back. She held her arms out and dropped gracefully to her knees. Her lustrous hair fell over her face in a shining curtain. Had I not known how much she wanted to kill me, I might have thought she was an angel. The wings that burst from her back told a different story.

They curled around her like a shield of dove-grey feathers, their tips brushing the floor. Judging by the show she made of her extra appendages, air combat was Lysiani's specialty. Sure enough, instead of simply standing back up, she launched herself up toward the ceiling. Her wings snapped open like the arms of a kite.

"Crazy bitch," I muttered.

She banked to the left and sped toward me, setting up for a fly-by. To me, that just made her an easier target.

I spoke too soon. She came at me like a ballistic missile, her huge wings set to dive. The rake of her talons nearly dragged me off my feet.

"Son of a bitch!" I shouted, mostly to mitigate the spread of white-hot pain that came a moment after she struck. Whirling around to track her, I held the *Gladius Solis* high and horizontal, like a samurai's blade.

She rushed at me again and again with remarkable speed.

Lysiani was a force unlike any I had known. Even the harpies were little more than pigeons compared to the eagle like ferocity with which she cut through the air.

So it was time to even the playing field.

I waited for my moment, then as Lysiani went streaming by, I sidestepped her trajectory and slashed to the side. A cloud of feathers exploded along the sword's cutting edge.

The goddess wavered in the air, shrieking with rage. She'd intended to pull up after buzzing me, but the hit on her wing devastated her balance. I got to watch her crash land on the hard marble floor of the vault, narrowly avoiding the pedestal and the drill.

Now that she was no longer fully in control of the LIGHT, she seemed to fear it. It was a weakness I intended to exploit to the fullest. As she struggled to regain position, I ignored her in favor of a closer inspection of the pedestal and the drill, as much as I could manage with all the glowing.

"This doesn't look very sturdy," I remarked. I swung my sword casually at the pedestal, taking a large chunk out of the bass. The drill teetered slightly.

"Don't touch it, you fool!" Lysiani's voice was shrill with tension and unspent rage. She readjusted her wings, and I saw that one of them was now missing a fair slice of its feathers. "You are ignorant of its strength. Step away."

"Like this?" I pushed the sword in deeper.

The harpy goddess's eyes widened. "Step away!" There was no hiding the panic in her voice. "One mistake, and we will all be killed!"

"That's funny." I put out a hand and touched the surface

of the pedestal. It thrummed with energy buildup. "Too bad I'm only Human. We're very accident prone."

I gave the platform a gentle shove and the platform bent slightly at the pressure. The drill rocked on its base.

"*No!*" Lysiani rushed me in a hail of feathers. Her long legs made short work of the enormous vault—I had only a second or two to prepare my attack. She reached to shove me away, and as she did so, I drove the sword deep into the flesh of her upper thigh. Time slowed for just that instant, granting me the rare opportunity to savor my vengeance.

Like always, the blade passed clean through organic material, but I still wrenched it free. Scarring even one part of her body gave me enormous satisfaction. Screaming, she twisted away. More feathers fell in clumps. Her right wing half-dragged along the floor.

"Weird," I said, tailing her as she tried to scuttle away. "I figured you'd be the biggest challenge, but your offspring I killed a couple hours ago put up a way better fight than this."

The goddess kicked viciously at me, aiming to tear at my legs with her spiked heels. I planted Kronin's sword deep in the center of the injured wing. Her whole long body went rigid with the pain. When I took the sword out, she fell back, gasping.

"It is the sword, not you. *You* are nothing."

"We'll see about that. Maybe this will relight your cold, dead heart." Taking the time to line up my shot, I reared back as if I was about to throw it. This monster, more than all the others before, needed to stay down.

A familiar, two-part racking sound was what stopped me.

"Don't do anything stupid," said Silas Monk. He held a twelve-gauge shotgun, and although it was certainly nothing to scoff at, I could tell by the way the barrel weaved that his grip was amateur and unsteady. Too bad with a shotgun, he barely needed to aim to shred me to pieces. "I'm not much of a gunman. I don't want to shoot you."

"Shoot her!" Lysiani commanded. "By order of your Goddess Queen, shoot her!"

Hesitantly, Monk raised the gun. His thumb wavered on the safety for a minute until I heard it click off. Unwilling to risk waiting another second, I grabbed the chunk of metal I had cut from the drill-base and hurled it overhand at him.

He flinched at the same time that he fired, driving the shot wide. I was too focused on him to notice Lysiani had gotten up behind me. She sank her claws into my shoulders and took flight on her jacked-up wings.

My shoulders were in agony. "You're an asshole!" I hollered. "Put me down or drop me. I don't care which!" When that failed to get a response, I started hacking one-handed at any part of her that I could reach. But she was healing; I felt the magic working beneath her skin. Even the burns from Kronin's blade dissolved quickly into new flesh.

My upper hand was fading fast. I tried not to let myself panic, but I knew if I let her get back to full strength, she would likely finish me then and there. Down below, the LIGHT drill still sat collecting energy.

That was the last trick up my sleeve.

As she flew higher, I reached up with one hand and

grabbed ahold of Lysiani's robe. Then I stabbed upward with the sword, attacking the arms that held me.

She screamed as she released me from her grasp, but I kept my grip on her robe.

The pain of my attack and the sudden shift in weight threw her off balance. We began to plummet toward the ground.

As we fell, she lashed out at me and I at her. We tumbled together, a blur of fire and fury. There were only seconds to prepare. With all my strength, I pulled, trying to get on top of her, keeping her body between me and the drill that was waiting for us down below.

I barely felt the explosion when we hit. One second I was hanging onto Lysiani for dear life, the next I was flying through the air, the world spinning around me. My whole back struck the wall with a resounding thud. There was a moment of ringing calm. Right after that, the wall I'd hit crumbled on top of me.

The silence under the debris was curiously muted, not unlike being underwater. I could still breathe, but my legs were pinned and so was half my torso. The *Gladius Solis* was buried in my right hand. I was terrifyingly stuck.

Do not panic, Victoria. Call on your sword.

In the heat of the fight, I'd forgotten about Marcus. His voice calmed me and stopped my heart from hammering out of my chest.

A breath in, a breath out.

The blade.

It obliterated the rocks above it immediately. I used the tip to carve a doorway out of the debris. The air that rushed in was dusty, tinted with hints of chemicals and burning plastic. I freed my arms, planted them on the floor, and heaved my way out of the concrete prison.

The vault was a mess. Where the pedestal with the drill had stood, there was only a blackened square surrounded by the blast pattern of the explosion. Most of the walls were missing chunks and marred by soot and ashes. I wondered vaguely if Monk was okay.

No immediate signs of him surfaced, but, of course, Lysiani burst from a fortification of rubble the moment she heard me. Debris turned into shrapnel from the sheer force of her entrance. I shielded my head.

"You." She glowered as if this had been solely my fault. "Where is Monk?" A long arm snaked in a flash toward my throat, but I caught her wrist just in time. The tendons flexed beneath her skin as she strained to overpower me, her hand inching closer to its goal.

I bore down.

"Hell if I know. I didn't see him before we all got blown sky-high." I smirked. "Are you just now realizing how fucked you are if he's dead? You don't know how any of his shit actually works, do you?"

Her talons swiped for my heart. I struck back with the flat of my sword. The blow knocked her to the side, sending her unbalanced ass to the floor. When she fanned her wings up, thrashing, the wall of wind beat me backwards with a force that took me by surprise. The gale wasn't enough to prevent me from severing her flight feathers, consigning her to the ground. This did not make those wings as useless as I hoped. She flapped them at me with the fury of a thousand storms, hurling curses from between her teeth. The wind rose to a whining howl.

"The strength is the sword's," she seethed again. Her words cut through the rushing air. "Not yours. Never yours!"

"Yeah, you said that one already. It doesn't seem to matter, does it?" Gripping the hilt overhand, I pushed forward and gouged out a slash in each wing, so large that I knew she'd be grounded for good—and maybe she'd stop calling up a damn tornado every second. She screeched. Her fierce rhythm faltered.

But she still managed to club me in the head with the bony top ridge of a wing. I reeled back, dazed as she made her escape. Both wings dragged limply behind her.

I climbed to my feet, ready to finish this thing, when a weak voice stopped me in my tracks.

"Help," Monk whimpered. "Please."

I turned to see the scientist in the firm grasp of a certain sun-glassed, man in black.

A knife bit at the soft skin of Monk's throat.

Brax pressed down on the knife until a thin rivulet of blood trickled from its underside. "Yes," he said, a little smugly. "I think our friend here really needs it."

26

"We're definitely not friends, Abraxzael," I said. "I need Monk alive, and if you're not going to cooperate, then we've got problems."

He seemed so taken aback by the use of his real name that he almost dropped Monk straight to the floor. The mirrored sunglasses focused intently on me. "So, you finally found me out. I have to say, that takes a certain amount of guts. Most people don't have 'em."

I smirked. "I got 'em for days, man. Which means I'm not going anywhere. You're not taking Monk out of my sight."

"I'll make a deal with you. Drop the sword, and I'll consider letting this puny man go."

"Not gonna happen."

He shrugged. "Then we're at an impasse."

"Don't I get a say in all this," Monk whimpered.

We both glared at him and shouted, "Shut up," simultaneously.

Vic, what are you going to do?

"I don't know," I muttered under my breath.

"Ah," Brax said with a smile. Talking to your invisible friend again? I'm sure he's the one who told you all about me. Brax the Betrayer, Criminal from Hell, or some shit like that. Kronin's lapdogs always have a flair for the dramatic."

"Says the guy in a trench coat and aviators."

He nodded. *"Touche."*

"And he told me that you're the lapdog. Let me guess, Lorcan sent you here, right? I thought the Marked hated the gods. I thought you fought a war just to free yourselves from them. Why the hell would you serve them now?"

"I'm what your people call a demon...we're not exactly known for our loyalty. My services simply go to the highest bidder, and I'm the best in the business. So they generally bid very high."

He flashed me a wide toothy grin. His yellow teeth were like small bricks. But there was something about what he said—or rather how he said it that didn't sit right with me. I'd been dealing with deception and manipulation all week, and I wasn't buying it.

"You're lying."

"What," he growled. His smile froze and became menacing.

I stood up straighter, lowering the sword by a couple inches. "It's all a lie. You, parading around like some cold blooded mercenary, but I don't believe it. You're nothing more than a pawn in this aren't you? What's Lorcan got over you?"

Brax opened his mouth to speak, but nothing came out.

He hemmed and hawed for a moment, then his shoulders relaxed. Letting go of Monk with one hand, he pulled down the collar of his shirt to show the very beginning of the chain tattoo I'd glimpsed before.

"I'm Marked," he said simply. "If you knew my name, you knew that already. You may not know that because of the brand, the Marked are essentially enslaved by the gods. We do what they say, or they send us back to hell." His smile was grim. "And I'm not going back to hell. Monk here is my ticket out."

"You guys gonna swap places? I don't think that's how the fairytale is supposed to go."

"Originally, I was supposed to bring back the weapon. But since the LIGHT seems to have gone the way of old broken things, I'll have to bring Monk back to build a new one."

"You... you can't just bring the pieces?" The trace of hope in Monk's voice was as sad as it was adorable.

"Not if you're the only one who knows how to put them together," Brax said. "Lorcan isn't into his own arts and crafts."

The name Lorcan perked my ears up. I was glad my bluff worked. Knowing now that Lysiani had slaughtered the majority of his vamps, the rat was probably in hiding, biding his time until he could figure out a next move.

"So you are working for Lorcan?" I asked.

Brax chuckled dryly. "Who isn't? Guy never does his own dirty work. Most of the gods, they were as surprised by old Kronin's death as he was. But Lorcan, he's a crafty son of a bitch. He's been planning this return from the beginning. This world will bow beneath him."

"Not if I can stop it first. You could help me."

Brax's laughter boomed throughout the ruined room. "You think because you got a few good licks in against that winged bitch that you can take Lorcan? There's not a god alive that holds a candle to what he can do. And if you think I'm going to get on his bad side, you're as crazy as those harpies."

"Better to die fighting than live as a coward."

Brax's large upper lip rose in a sneer. "Better to live as a coward than spend eternity in hell. Trust me princess. You don't know what you're up against. Now," he lowered the knife and wrapped his arm around Monk's neck. Then he started dragging the small man backward. "If you'll excuse me, I have a job to finish."

"Like hell you do!" The high pitched scream came from the across the room. All three of us looked in that direction, just in time to see a woman in a red dress pick up Monk's shotgun. I knew her instantly, despite the new, angry scarring over one side of her face.

What was she doing here?

"Eve?" Monk's voice was soft and stricken with horror. "What happened to you?"

She turned on him. "You know exactly what happened. And so do you!" This last part was directed at Brax as she turned the weapon toward them. "Why wouldn't I be here? Someone needs to pay for everything I've lost. You're the only one who seems to have the money." The shotgun cocked. "So, pay up."

"Whoa, whoa." Monk held his hands up. "Let's not get crazy here. I'm sorry about your face, Eve, but I don't owe you reparations. He's the one who broke into the hotel room with a flaming hammer."

"And yet, I'm not the one she wants to kill," Brax noted.

The whole scene was weird, to say the least. Whatever I had expected out of this last encounter, pseudo-family drama was not it. I almost felt like I should leave until they sorted it out, but then Eve exploded and drew us all in.

"It's his fault," she said, pointing a shaking finger at Monk. "Because he's the one who built the drill. He's the one who caught Lysiani's attention and made her give me away so I could keep him on our side. And he's the one who abandoned me like trash after I was ruined!" Tears brimmed at the corners of her eyes. "I did everything for you, Silas Monk! I taught you how to dress, how to talk. I helped you facilitate the last phases of production. I found investors. I made sure your dreams came true! And this is how I get repaid." She sniffled, on the brink of another breakdown.

"What?" I interrupted, confused. "You deserve a fresh start? After all the shit we've gone through here because of you? Call me crazy, but I don't think that's going to happen."

Eve broke down into slightly hysterical laughter that took all emotion out of her face when it subsided. "No. There's no starting over for me. It's too late."

27

THE RED DRESS flicked around Eve's feet as she paced the vault with a manic glint in her eye. She was the same woman I had seen at Monk's side during the gala event at SF Tech only a few days ago, but she wasn't that woman at all.

The burn scars reminded me of Rocco, but even beyond that, something had changed in her. Where she had been smug and self-satisfied, supremely confident in her own ability, now she was raging at a world that had failed her.

"Once upon a time, I was a beauty queen of great renown. *World* renown. Every week, it was somewhere different, somewhere new and exotic to explore. And everywhere I went, I had fans. People flocked to see me on the stage. They recognized me in the streets. Men fell over each other to buy me gifts, to be with me."

A real smile bloomed on her face as she described them, and she spun in blissful circles around the ruined vault like she was back on one of those stages. I kept my eyes on the shotgun, which pointed in my direction at the apex of every spin.

Eve's movements were too erratic to make a move on her. I had to hang back and keep my eye out for an opportunity to save Monk and myself. When the time came, Brax would be on his own.

Eve slowed, and the smile fell away. The lines around her eyes and face seemed to redraw themselves deeper than before.

"But it couldn't last," she said. "The days came and went, and that thrilling lifeblood stopped pumping through my veins. I aged out of the competition arena, losing my spot to younger, more vital girls. No one recognized me anymore, or if they did, it was fleeting. I haunted conversations in past tense: 'the girl who was.' My whole life was built on sand in the hourglass, and it all crumbled slowly away."

Her hands clenched tightly around the shotgun. I cringed, half expecting it to go off. Luckily, this crazy harpy still had enough sense in her charbroiled head to keep her finger off the trigger. Still, she was really taking advantage of her captive audience with this long confession. I racked my brain for a way to overpower her, if for no other reason than to put an end to this pathetic display.

"I got lonely," Eve continued. "Then, I got angry, and then I just got damn sad." An inscrutable expression passed over her face like a cloud. "Then I found Lysiani. Or rather, she found me."

"And you sold your body to her, just so you could look pretty again?" I shook my head. "Lady, you were messed up before you ever became a harpy."

Eve took a long time to answer that one. "It's more than my body. She asked for my soul. And I gladly gave it to her. Then, she made me beautiful." She faltered. "I gave up my soul for this. Now I'm nothing." Tears streamed unchecked down her cheeks, dripping off the scarred line of her lower jaw. She pointed the shotgun at Monk. "Do you know what that means, Silas? To have your life snuffed away in an instant? You're about to."

Monk backed off, sort of ducking behind Brax for protection. Brax just eyed the woman in red with a close cynicism.

"Eve, wait," I said, hoping to keep the shotgun from going off. Monk was still right there. Right in the line of fire.

"I've waited long enough."

The gun roared and threw her backward. Brax covered Silas Monk with the broad shelter of his body before buckling over at the waist amid a spray of blood. This was the chance I'd been waiting for. I sprang toward her, tackling the weapon out of her hands. She fell to the side, and it clattered between us. I kicked it out of her reach as her long fingers scrabbled for a hold.

"That was the wrong choice, Eve," I said.

The skin on her face was sagging, spidering over with blotches and veins. The wings that sprouted from her shoulders were rumpled and dull, but I knew better than to be fooled by her body's state of disrepair. The sunken eyes in her skull glinted with malice.

"It's over," I told her. "Just let go."

She lunged at me, making a high, keening wail. I caught her, and her wings beat in my face. With pure strength, I threw her over my shoulder where she landed in a rough heap, struggling to get back up. I didn't want to fight close quarters with her, but she refused to allow distance between us. Locked in a grapple on the floor, she seized my sword and it flew backward over her head.

"Dammit," I shouted.

Eve produced an impish smile that didn't belong to her new, tired face. She curled her legs between us and kicked, forcing me off of her. She jumped to her feet, but I was faster than her, and I grabbed her wing by the stem, jerking her backward. She fell hard against the marble floor. The crack of bone rang out like a shot. Ahead, I saw the outline of the hilt she'd wrestled away from me.

Her smile was weak this time, lopsided. The words that left her mouth slurred together. "Can't blame me for trying, can you?"

"Yeah," I said. "Actually, I can." I stood over her, my foot on her chest.

Her bedraggled form slumped down into the floor. I almost didn't hear the reply.

"They loved me. They all loved me."

With her last ounce of venom, she tried to fake me out and bring me down on top of her outstretched claws.

My hand shot out in the direction of the fallen hilt. "*Gladius Solis!*"

The sword rocketed into my hand. I summoned the blade just in time to block the ragged points of her nails. The heat grew blisters on her papery skin.

Eve bared her teeth, but it was just a formality now. The sword cast her features in a weird fiery glow as the blade disappeared through her chest. She looked incongruously fragile from this angle, little more than an old woman clothed in the red trappings of beauty. Her pale eyes went wide, she drew one final, heaving breath, and then was still.

There was no triumph in her death. Only emptiness.

When I turned around, I realized why.

Eve's last shotgun blast tore straight through Brax and caught Silas Monk in the chest. Monk still lay where he'd fallen. His eyes were fixed and staring, and the wound in his torso was unsurvivable. I walked over and placed my hand on his neck. He was already getting cold. A pool of blood coagulated around him, and as I rose to my feet, I thought that at least he wouldn't have to deal with the cleanup.

But where was Brax? An ominous silence reigned in the vault. I stayed where I was, listening for any sign of the missing Marked. His blood was still pooled with Monk's, but only the inventor had died here.

Be cautious, Marcus advised. *The Marked are extremely difficult to kill. If Abraxzael's corpse is missing, he is still alive.*

"Hey, Marcus. Can I ask you something?"

Anything, as long as you're all right.

I sat back on my heels, emptying the air from my lungs.

"Do you ever have something positive to say?

2 8

Back in New York, I sat glumly on the mattress in my loft, alone and brooding. There was a newspaper on the table, and even from the low vantage point of the bed, I could see the frontpage headline: **TECH GURU SILAS MONK FOUND DEAD**.

I didn't want to look at it, but my eyes couldn't stay away from either the words or the full-color photograph underneath them. He was beaming in it, obviously on the red carpet of some big event, and I kept wondering if he had known Eve when the picture was taken. Was that the real Silas Monk, or the one she had built with false confidence and black magic?

Maybe it didn't really make a difference in the end, but it sort of did to me. I wanted to believe that a person who gifted so much amazing shit to an otherwise mediocre world needed the influence of a harpy to end up dead in the middle of his own dream come true. I wanted to believe that because Silas Monk didn't deserve to die.

Not everything was a loss. I had made a friend, and an ally, in Namiko. We had parted ways with brief goodbyes, but I had a feeling that it wasn't the last time I would hear from her—or her from me. SplitScreen, as I first knew her, had plenty of connections that I guessed might come in handy soon enough.

But, I was still pissed about losing the drill. "That was our trump card," I complained to Marcus one afternoon a few days after. "It would have been cool if we could've used it."

It seemed right to be able to honor Silas's legacy by shooting a huge-ass laser at the next crop of monsters. Something told me he would have approved.

We do not need another 'trump card' when we have you.

Those kinds of compliments never failed to make me smile. Call it juvenile, but I loved the idea of being any kind of secret weapon, let alone a secret weapon against the gods. And the more I got myself into hotter and hotter water, the more it seemed like an apt description.

"I guess I did kick a goddess's ass," I said, exuding modesty from my very pores. "It was pretty easy." In my head, I was brushing off my shoulders, but I knew the gesture would be wasted on Marcus.

Do not get ahead of yourself, Marcus said. I could hear the smile in his voice, even though he didn't have lips or a face. *There are gods, and then there are* gods. *Lysiani ranks fairly low on that list.*

"Ugh." The cat hopped into my lap and started shouting her hunger, so I got up to take care of it, relieved to have something mundane to do. "Aren't you supposed to be building my confidence? Telling me I can do anything?"

You wield the weapon of the only singular king our world has ever had, and you want me to reconfirm that you can do anything?

"Yeah, you're right." I grinned. "I guess I *am* pretty much a badass." I put some dry kibble into the cat's bowl and set it on the floor for her. "Can we finally talk about this Brax guy, though? You've been sketchy about him ever since he showed up."

The Marked are dangerous and untrustworthy, Marcus said, as he had every time I brought it up. *"I have no doubt that he still lives. Perhaps he just feels you may still be of use to him somewhere down the line.*

I reached into the fridge and poured myself a glass of juice. The beer bottles on the bottom shelf always tempted me, but recent events had me wanting to run my ship a little tighter.

Monk was the first real, personal casualty in my new life, and I'd be lying if I said it didn't freak me out a little. It was a grim reminder of what I was up against, and now, I was searching for all the specks of light I could possibly find in the darkness. Including the ones with chain tattoos all over their bodies.

"I'm just saying, he didn't seem like a bloodthirsty warmonger to me. Definitely a guy who's willing and able to skew ethics in order to get shit done, but let's be real—that's me, too. That's probably a lot of people. It's not a perfect world."

That is true, but it is worth noting that the Marked were not created with ethics at the forefront in terms of priorities. If they are not perfect slaves willing to execute their god's most brutal orders, then they are consumed with the fires of self-

righteous vengeance and do not think beyond their own grati-fication.

"Again, you've basically just described me in the early years of my vendetta against Rocco Durant," I said. "I see the point you're making Marcus. I really do. But some-times people become that way for reasons that aren't auto-matically apparent. There might be more to Brax than what you think about him. That's all I'm saying."

You may be correct about that. However, I lack information in which to put my faith. It seems to be that many of the Forgotten did not receive the same kinds of sensitization which humankind's theoretical Creator has provided us.

"Marcus, are you monster-racist?" It was rude to poke fun at something that made him so serious, but I just couldn't let it slide. "Come on, I'm sure there are nice vampires out there. I just haven't met the right one yet."

I said many; I did not say all. My ogre acquaintance at the club we attended is a prototypical example of creatures in his class. There are always exceptions, but they are few and far between. Even more so lately, it seems.

"You don't think the Marked, as a race, are exceptions? Seems like that's exactly what they were made to be."

He thought about that one for a while. *Your mind continues to surprise me, Victoria. On rare occasion, anyway. I confess I had never considered the question from that angle before.*

"Don't say I never taught you anything." I took a sip of my juice. "You think he'll really be back?"

Abraxzael? I have no doubt your paths will cross again. It is evident that you have captured his interest for whatever reasons he may have.

"Maybe he's lonely," I suggested.

He was made to be lonely.

"Wow, okay. Now I want you guys to meet in person, just so I can see you fight."

No. That means someone else would receive the honor of killing him in order to let him face me.

I had never seen Marcus carrying a chip on his shoulder, let alone one against a semi-demon slave warrior, Whatever history lay beneath that, I desperately wanted to know it. But I also knew not to push Marcus on a sensitive topic. So, I made a mental note to keep an eye out for guys who wore trench coats and sunglasses all the time.

"Hey, Marcus?"

Yes? He knew something criminally stupid was coming. He had to.

"Do you think they all dress like that, or is Brax just the coolest one?"

I just remembered that tomorrow's training begins at four in the morning.

"Man, I'm just joking around with you. You don't have to murder me in retaliation." As I said that, I happened to look over and see Silas Monk's face on the newspaper. Everything I'd just said suddenly felt irreverent and weird.

Do you wish to attend the funeral?

"Half yes, half no. Maybe a quarter yes, three-quarters no." I sighed. "I want to go because I was there and because I only sort of knew him. It would be cool to get a bigger picture of who he was. But at the same time, I think the picture might be too big, if that makes sense. Does it mean something if I'm a mourner instead of a friend?" I shrugged. "Maybe that's a stupid thing to worry about in times like these, but I think about it sometimes when I can't sleep. And you know what else I think about?"

What?

"How I'm afraid of the way it would look if I went there. Not the way people would look at me—they're free to think however they want—but I think the way Monk's funeral would appear to me is like the view from the top of the first hill on a rollercoaster. The moment when you realize the only way from here on out is down."

EPILOGUE

Even after all her plans had sunken like a battleship lost at sea, the mansion remained. It was a gift from one of her now fallen angels. Lysiani was grateful for its extravagant comfort as the front door locked behind her. She caught a glimpse of her reflection in the hall mirror and recoiled slightly. Her worst fear confirmed: she looked as dreadful as she felt.

It had been so long since she'd felt pain like this—both from physical trauma and from failure. How dare that girl with the god-king's sword come meddling in the affairs of gods! She would need to be dealt with, as soon as Lysiani's body was restored. But no sooner; this concession, the goddess had to make.

She flicked on the light and screamed.

Standing in the entrance to the sitting room, Lorcan smiled. "We meet again at last, Lysiani."

The goddess bared her teeth and talons, lunging for him. "You are not welcome here, you grim court jester!"

Lorcan simply batted her out of midair. She was so little to him, a feather against a storm. He stepped toward her writhing form and knelt upon her chest, bringing his face down close to hers. "Bold of you to call me a jester, fool." She flinched, which satisfied him immensely. "I need not remind you of your many errors, but as long as I've got you here...I figure I might as well. What idiocy it was to try and acquire the LIGHT for yourself. If you would need it to defeat a god like me—and you would—then it is more than you deserve." His pale eyes narrowed into slits.

"I deserve the world," she growled. "More than a back-stabbing snake like you."

"You are nothing, Lysiani. Nothing more than a simpleton whose vanity and pride outweigh what little common sense she has. It was a mistake to kill my subjects. A mistake you will sorely regret."

"How could it have been a mistake if it was so easy?" She smiled thinly. "Look at you, Lorcan. Thinking you're so high and mighty. The man I see tonight is a far cry from the one I knew so long ago. How strong you were back then. How virile." She lifted a slender finger to trace the line of his jaw. "And what are you now?"

Lorcan laughed dryly. "As if your tricks would have any effect on me, woman. Have you seen yourself? That little girl and her talking necklace made a mockery of you. I saw the whole thing—the scientist had cameras throughout his lab." He sighed. "It is all a shame, isn't it? Not that Silas Monk is dead—I had no real need for him anyway. But Abraxzael...for him, my hopes were high. He was there you know. Standing over the human's body as she dispatched with your last pet. He could have crushed her like the insect she is. But instead he just turned around and left. Perhaps he thought I would welch on our deal, but his freedom was waiting if he brought me the sword. Instead, he chooses to run?" An edge of steel hardened his gaze. "A pity." Then his countenance cleared. "No matter. I shall hunt him down like the animal he is and return him to eternal torment soon enough."

Lysiani drew a shallow breath. "Is that my fate as well, Lorcan? Or is it the cold embrace of death?"

The god arched his eyebrows at his captive quarry. "Death? No, no, beautiful Lysiani. You are far too valuable to kill. I have great plans for you and your...gifts. But torment," a Cheshire smile spread across Lorcan's face, contorting his sallow features. "Yes, there will be torment."

Dear Fabulous Readers,

Right now, I feel like I am underwater, popping meds for a head cold that has kicked me in the face and is standing over me laughing. But you know what? I'm laughing right back.

Other than the clogged ears and pounding temples, I'm as happy as an author can get, because a few hours ago, Forgotten Gods (Book 1) snatched its first bestseller tag on Amazon and is hanging out with a fistful of five-star reviews!

Take that head cold!

And you know what? It is all because of you, the readers. You are all freaking awesome. Thank you for reading, reviewing, and engaging. It means the world to us!

In my last notes, I told you all that I started writing for an audience of one: my sweet daughter Simone. Even if she was the only person in the world that ever read those quirky books about a bunch of kids stranded mysteriously on an island, every painstaking word I punched out on the keyboard was totally worth it.

And she read them. And then she read them again and again.

Simone came up with the craziest questions about those kids, what happened to them, and how it all would end. We'd lay in her bed at night and discuss our favorite characters, funniest lines, and who she would "ship". (That's kid lingo for who she would put together in a relationship. I had to ask.)

Now, years later, I get to write stories for thousands of fans. I chat with some of you about favorite characters, you post funniest lines on Facebook, and some of you ask me, "How will it all end?"

Being a part-time author ain't easy. I burn the midnight oil. Right now, most of my friends are in bed, binging Netflix, or finishing their second drink at the local bar. And I'm here, at my little table in my quiet kitchen writing to you.

And you know what?

Just like writing for Simone, every painstaking word of these books, every hour of sleep lost, every show not watched, and yes, even every drink not imbibed at the local dive is totally worth it!

Once I'm done with these notes, I'm turning to wrap up edits on Forgotten Gods, book 3. Lee and I (AKA ST Branton) aren't sure what it's going to be called yet (hey, we need to get on that, Lee), but the story is pretty great.

Vic is growing in her role as hero, and she finds herself in a new place developing new friendships that will help her conquer another Forgotten God! It is fast paced and superfun, and the only thing it made me wish is that we could create the stories faster. I CAN'T WAIT to see where it all goes.

Speaking of which, I better get to it. The clock is ticking, and the gods are coming!

Cheers,
Chris

Here's my big PS for this book: Lee and I are becoming pretty prolific as authors, and we have a decent backlist of books as well. If you want to make sure you NEVER miss a release, a giveaway, or one-day fan pricing, please take a minute to sign up for our mailing list.

You can do it here:
https://www.subscribepage.com/smokeandsteelnews

So, great news in the Barbant household. Baby Barbant has learned how to stand on his own. It's an awesome milestone, and stressful as hell. I now have to baby proof my house two feet higher than before. At the rate he's growing, my top cabinets will be locked down tight by the summer.

I'm a first-time dad, so everytime something like this happens, I freak out a little bit. It's cliche, I know. I'm the parent from every diaper/laundry/band-aid commercial. It's just that they change so fast, and I have so little control over when and how it's going to happen.

Why didn't anyone tell me that beforehand? You all are supposed to be looking out for me.

When I started writing, I thought I'd have total control over my characters, too. I mean, what are they going to do? Talk back? I CONTROL THE KEYBOARD. SAY NO ONE MORE TIME, AND YOU'LL SPEND ALL OF NEXT BOOK WADING THROUGH A SEWER.

My wife just stopped me to confirm that I don't discipline Baby Barbant like I do the characters. Of course not, dear ;)

The funny thing is, I have way less control over our fiction than I think. And I'm not just talking about the fact that Chris comes along and deletes all my best one-liners [Did you hear the one about the overworked muffler? It was exhausted!!!]

It's just that sometimes a story goes in a wildly different direction than you meticulously plan. And that requires pushing your characters in previously unaccounted for directions. And you know what? The story turns out way better for it.

Another thing that helps the story is you all. If it takes a village to raise a child, then it takes a damn country to write a book. I wanted to thank everyone who helped get this project out the door, especially the folks over on the Forgotten Gods Facebook Group. Once I finish these author notes, I'm going to get back to wrapping book 3-- which was majorly influenced by discussions happening online.

So, if you're digging this series, come join us. Well, first go leave an Amazon review, then come join us. You can let us know what you loved and what you hated and what you're hoping to see in future books. You can help answer the dozens of questions that I have. And you can maybe give me some child rearing advice? Like seriously, the kid is a monster. But the good kind that lets me snuggle him after he's ripped out half my beard.

Anyway, I'm starting to get mushy and rambly which is

a bad combination. Next think you know I'll be crying over the keyboard talking about that time Chris gave me a bad grade in grad school. Not pretty.

For Kronin!

Lee